THE OUT-HAUL

The mare must tire soon, and Celia was determined to stick on her back at any cost. She could see the crest of the hill about a hundred yards ahead, and she remembered vaguely that horses did not like galloping downhill – or was it people who did not like horses to gallop downhill . . .

She clung, and tried not to think about the hardness of the tarmac flashing past below her eyes, just slightly to her right, nor of the possibility of holes in the grass verge. All her concentration was spent on staying on, her muscles inflamed by a tiny picture of a white-crash-helmetted person in a smart tweed jacket lying senseless in the middle of the road. It was not going to be her.

Also by Alannah Hopkin in Sphere Books:

A JOKE GOES A LONG WAY IN THE COUNTRY

The Out-haul

ALANNAH HOPKIN

SPHERE BOOKS LIMITED

First published in Great Britain by
Hamish Hamilton Ltd, 1985

Published by Sphere Books Ltd, 1986
27 Wright's Lane, London W8 5SW

TRADE
MARK

Set in Plantin

Printed and bound in Great Britain by
Collins, Glasgow

We can tell whether we are happy by the sound of the wind. It warns the unhappy man of the fragility of his house, hounding him from shallow sleep and violent dreams. To the happy man it is the song of his protectedness: its furious howling concedes that it has power over him no longer.

Theodor Adorno
Minima Moralia

Dedication

For Pix

AUGUST

Celia could never understand how or why she persuaded Nick to take her to Bally C that summer. In retrospect she came to believe that the arbitrary choice which was to have such a dramatic influence on the course of her life had been dictated to her by some combination of powers beyond her comprehension. Sometimes when Celia thought about the random chain of events which took her back to Bally C she almost became mystic, a state of mind quite alien to her normal practical self.

Bally C has one main street which winds along a cliff top at the base of Mount Cornelia and then turns inland, running downhill so that you'd never know that the north end of Bally C was near the coast at all. Nick parked the car beside the ruined granite castle which gives the place its name – Ballycashlinacosta – and walked over to read the historical information written on a small rusty plaque.

Another steep curving street runs down to the quay. Nick and Celia walked down to inspect two small trawlers tied up alongside. Several yachts were moored in the shelter of the pier. Nick and Celia stood and watched a man and a woman disembark from one of the yachts and row ashore in a rubber dinghy with a large plastic container balanced between them.

'That's the life,' said Nick.

'Come on,' said Celia, 'I'll show you the rest of the town.'

It only took five minutes. Bally C is not really a town at all, just an overgrown village. It has a large Catholic church, a smaller one for the other crowd, a school, a community hall, a post office, a bank, one hotel, about half a dozen shops, a garage and nine bars, some of which are also general stores.

Celia had known Bally C in the boom years of the early 'seventies when quarter acre plots and stone-built ruins and quite undesirable terraced cottages on the main street were being sold off as holiday homes. Her parents-in-law had built a bungalow overlooking Roaring Water Bay about two miles outside Bally C, and she and her husband Liam used to borrow it for holidays. She had not been back since her divorce, but she knew that her in-laws were among the lucky few who had managed to sell their house before the slump. Many buildings in the village now bore weathered For Sale and To Let signs, including the craft commune and the three restaurants which Bally C had accumulated at the height of its popularity with tourists.

'Must be cheap to buy a place here these days,' said Nick.

'Yes. But look at what it cost us to get here.'

'Don't remind me. By the way, we'd better change some money.'

'Okay. Then we'll go and see Lily.'

Lily ran a small bar and general store in a corner shop at the sheltered north end of Bally C. She was a quiet woman of late middle-age with a gentle manner and a sweetness of character most unexpected in an unmarried female publican. But, after a lifetime of bar work she could be firm when the occasion called for it. She had inherited the business from her mother, and made no attempt to redecorate or keep up with the times beyond installing a television in her back room. Those who appreciate the shabby charms of such old-fashioned establishments provided Lily with a loyal network of customers. She had her quota of Bally C locals and her share of such tourists as there were, but her clientele consisted mainly of people known as 'blow-ins' or 'settlers', labels applied to any resident who was not a born native of Bally C.

On that sunny morning in late August, Lily was sitting on her tall stool behind the bar watching her cousin Pake through the top part of the window as he rolled out empty beer kegs to the brewery truck. Pake did most of the heavy work around the place and filled in behind the bar on those rare occasions when Lily took a day off.

Nick and Celia came out of the bank and stood for a moment looking across the road towards Lily's. Lily watched with interest as Celia put her arms around Nick and kissed him on the mouth. She looked familiar to Lily. It was the pony tail of dark wavy hair, tied high on her head that Lily remembered, not the bright pink T shirt nor the ample hips encased in tight faded jeans. She caught a glimpse of Celia's face, a good-natured one with lively eyes under a thick fringe of hair, and an easy smile. The smile jogged something in Lily's memory . . . four, five years ago . . . But this one seemed bigger, not exactly fat, but certainly not a skinny slip of a thing like a lot of them. This one was a fine figure of a woman.

It was the man who was causing Lily confusion. A tall, grey-haired fellow with a neat grey beard and a yellowish face which was younger than his greyness would lead you to expect. Something foreign about him, and he was keeping company with *her* . . .

Lily remembered at exactly the moment that Celia walked through the open door of the bar.

'Hallo, my dear,' she said, walking towards the door with a hand outstretched in welcome. 'It's Celia, isn't it? It's a long time since we've seen you in here.'

'Lily! You still remember me?'

'I do a'course,' said Lily. 'You used to stay with the Kellys when they had the house above.'

'That's right. But it was years ago. I wasn't sure you'd still know me.' She smiled at the man beside her.

'Lily, I want you to meet Nick.'

They shook hands. 'Celia's told me a lot about you,' he said.

'Is it your first time in Bally C?'

'Yes. My first time in Ireland in fact. We just got off the plane two hours ago.'

'Well, well, well. In that case, *céad míle fáilte*.'

Nick felt awkward with the extended pleasantries and wondered how to order a drink without seeming impersonal. Lily anticipated him by going behind the bar.

'And what can I get for you?'

'A pint of Guinness please and . . .' he turned to Celia.

'A bloody Mary. For old times' sake. Lily makes the best bloody Marys in West Cork.'

'Well, and it has been a long time now, hasn't it?' said Lily. 'Five years or more. I thought you'd abandoned us completely.'

'Five, six . . . I honestly don't know,' said Celia, 'and I really should.'

That was because on her last visit to Bally C her marriage to Liam Kelly had finally ended. She had left him alone in his parents' bungalow and returned to Dublin to clear her things out of their flat, and move to London to start life again on her own.

'You know I split up with Liam, don't you?'

'I do a'course. Ice, my dear?'

'Yes please. The lot.'

Lily poured Worcester sauce, Tabasco and celery salt into the drink then turned back to spoon the creamy head off the porter and slowly top up Nick's pint glass.

'Are you staying in Bally C or just passing through?'

'We're hoping to stay for a couple of nights. At a B & B probably, but we haven't booked anything yet. If it comes to the worst I suppose there's always the Hilton.'

The Bally C Hotel was referred to by that name as a result of the local custom of bestowing nicknames, usually absurd or sarcastic but always loyally affectionate, on any suitable target.

'I've heard they do a nice B & B above the Penny Farthing,' said Lily, 'I wouldn't go near the Hilton if I were you. He's as bad as ever.'

'Dermot's still running it?'

'He is, what's left of it, as best he can. They dried him out last winter above in the hospital, and he was as charming as could be for a week, but now he's as bad as ever again. Poor man, they shouldn't let him near the drink. He should learn to stay on the dry.'

She looked up at the couple who had walked through the open door as she spoke, and nodded at them.

'You're not talking about Ben, are you?' said the woman. 'I've been telling him that ever since I met him.'

'Of course not, Clarissa, my dear,' said Lily. 'It's Dermot above I was . . .'

Lily's reply was drowned by a shout from the man behind Clarissa.

'Hell, Lily, you know as well as I do that there is one very good reason why I'll never go on the dry.'

He was a middle-aged man, barrel-chested with an American accent and a very loud voice. After a short dramatic pause he continued: 'If I ever go on the dry, you, my dear Lily, will go *broke*.' He slammed his fist on the bar to emphasise the last word.

The woman called Clarissa sat up at the bar and produced a chequebook.

'You don't mind do you Lily? We just missed the bank.'

'That's quite alright my dear.'

Clarissa was tall and thin with very long straight brown hair hanging loose down her back. Celia looked enviously at her long brown legs, and promised herself that by next summer she would lose enough weight to be able to wear shorts.

'Hello there,' Ben smiled at Nick and Celia, and did a double-take on Celia.

'Hey, haven't I seen you someplace before?'

'Christ, what a line,' said the woman called Clarissa in strident English Home Counties tones.

'In here,' said Celia.

He hit himself on the head with the palm of his hand.

'But a'course! Aren't you that crazy broad who ran out on Liam Kelly? You've put on some flesh since then.' He looked at Celia appreciatively and went on, 'Hey, whatever happened to Liam?'

His enthusiastic question was addressed to the room in general. Nick studied his pint, and Celia, offended, as always, by the reference to her ample proportions, did not bother to reply.

Silence.

'Oh, hell, I'm sorry,' said the American. 'Gross of me, I'm feeling gross so I act gross. Lily, fill a drink all round. Ben Finnegan.' He stretched his hand out to Nick.

'Nick Rosenberg.'

'Celia.'

'Clarissa Lyons, in case anyone's interested.'

The name rang a faint bell in Nick's mind.

'You're English too,' he said, turning away from Ben who was giving Celia an apologetic hug.

'Obviously.' Clarissa was not fond of making concessions to conventional good manners.

'It's just that your name seems familiar but I can't quite place it . . .'

Optimism lightened Clarissa's voice.

'Do you read poetry?'

'Yes. I teach it too.' The words slipped out of his mouth before he had time to think.

'Gosh. You *teach* poetry. Hey, Ben, did you hear that – he *teaches* poetry . . .'

'Clarissa Lyons!' said Nick. 'I *have* read you.' He hoped she would not ask where or when.

'Oh, that's made my day,' she said, suddenly losing her sourness. 'I hardly ever get a chance to talk shop, and I love to. I'm working on a new collection at the moment, but I haven't published any new verse for years. Where do you teach?'

'London. Kings.'

'Aha. In that case you must work with that old bastard Henry Marsh . . .'

Clarissa went off on a long and scurrilous anecdote, and there was no stopping her. Nick stared at her with surprise as he listened. He had not expected her to be so young – early thirties, he guessed – nor so good-looking. Her skin was tanned and glowing and she wore no make-up. She had the kind of high-cheekboned, wide-mouthed face that used to be popular on fashion models in the late 'sixties, and a model's lean, uncurving figure.

Ben watched Clarissa's animated monologue with a certain pride.

'You haven't met Clarissa before, have you?' he asked Celia.

'No. This is my first time back since I left Liam.'

'She turned up one Easter, two, three years ago, touring on a bicycle. She kinda liked it, so she stayed.'

'Great,' Celia laughed. It was a typical Bally C story.

'She's working on a new collection of verse. Three hundred poems. She's somewhere up in the two hundred and eighties right now.'

'Oh.' This seemed a somewhat bizarre activity to Celia. 'What about you? Are you still writing?'

'Yeah, when I'm not shooting or sailing. The usual, one crappy thriller a year. And what have you been up to?'

'Tefeling.'

Ben looked blank. 'What the hell is that?'

'Teaching English as a Foreign Language. TEFLing. It's incredibly horribly boring. I started when I was with Liam because we needed the money, and I stayed with it when I left him because I wanted to travel. So then I travelled, fine, London, Spain, Italy, Provence, then I went back to London to find a real job, something in publishing I thought. That was nearly two years ago, and I'm still looking. So meanwhile I TEFL.'

She frowned. She would have preferred to be able to describe her job in fewer words or at least to be able to make her dislike of it sound witty. Instead, every time she was asked, out came a tense, embittered speech which only served to remind her how much she hated it.

Ben showed no great interest in Celia's career problems, but asked again for news of Liam.

'He went to Canada and got into film-making, then he came back to Dublin. He's involved with some small company there. I think he's doing all right. We don't really bother to keep in touch, there doesn't seem much point.'

'There isn't,' said Ben, and began a story about his first ex-wife. Celia was pleased that Nick was also enjoying himself. Having persuaded him to travel so far for a weekend break she would feel responsible if he did not like Bally C.

On Sunday, their last afternoon, Nick and Celia drove out to the Mizen Head, a popular landmark at the tip of a nearby peninsula. The roads were almost deserted, just as they had been in the tourist brochure that Celia had produced to kindle Nick's interest in West Cork. They drove past old-fashioned conical stooks of hay drying in the sunshine, and through sleepy villages where all the houses were painted in different colours.

As they neared the mizen the landscape became rougher. Large grey boulders, some the size of half a house, were strewn over the hillside. There were no signs of cultivation, only sheep grazing.

'Look out for sheep on the road,' said Celia.

'It's beautiful,' said Nick.

They were alone at the Mizen Head. They walked together down the cliff path towards the light house in silence. As they got nearer Nick saw that the light house was built on a large rock separated from the mainland by a dizzying chasm of sheer sided black granite. A red-painted metal bridge built across the chasm led to the light house. They stopped at the locked gate of the bridge and stared down at the white spray crashing on to the rocks far below them.

There was a stiff breeze out on the headland which cut through Celia's T shirt chilling her in spite of the bright sunlight. She turned and left Nick staring at the towering light house across the bridge. She walked up the zig zag path along the cliff and back down the track towards the car.

When she reached the car she did not get in for shelter, but, attracted by the cries of a flock of swooping, gliding gulls, walked across the rough grass towards the cliff edge. There was no sheer drop: the grass sloped down and came to an end above a small bay which lay some sixty feet below the dark grey cliffs. She could not work out what was attracting the attention of the gulls, but stared at their regularly repeated manoeuvres, transfixed.

Part of her mind wandered back to Lily's, and the meeting with Ben and Clarissa, back to Bally C. She was seized by a strong utterly illogical longing to be back there. Pictures of towns and cities she had lived in, nomad-like, for the past six years flashed in front of her eyes like some manic travelogue, perverse and pointless and exhausting. But the travelogue had a final scene; it ended in Bally C. For a split second Celia was aware of Bally C as a place to live, not merely to visit. Bally C as home. She liked the idea, then shrugged it off as impossible, impractical, too wildly romantic.

As she reached the car she saw Nick walking up the cliff path towards her, waving his arms in the air, his white shirt flapping in the wind.

'Celia! I've just had a brainwave. Let's stay here! Let's rent a cottage in Bally C for my sabbatical and come back in September to stay!'

At first Celia was delighted with Nick's idea. Not only did it mean she could take a break from TEFLing, it also meant he had decided to leave his wife. For over six months now, Nick and Celia's relationship had been confined to Thursday evenings; a quick drink in the pub after work, then back to her flat until ten forty-five when the alarm clock reminded Nick to leave in time for the last train home. This was the first time he had gone so far as to take her away for the weekend, and now he was proposing that they set up house together, and in Bally C, of all places.

But back in Lily's, after a couple of celebratory drinks, small fears started to grow in Celia. She was awed by Nick's decision to leave his family in order to be with her. She had not thought his feelings for her were that strong: she saw herself as a pleasant, undemanding interlude in his weekly routine, not as a marriage wrecker. That role made her feel guilty. But then perhaps Nick would have left his wife even if Celia had not been around, though somehow she doubted it.

Then there was the question of her own independence. Since leaving her husband, Celia had realised that she was one of those rare people who, for most of the time, enjoy living alone. There were occasional moments of appalling loneliness, which made her acutely aware of the absence in her life: the lack of steady companionship and love. She visualised these moods as dark corners, and did her best to stay out of them. Such was the price of freedom. However, it was a price that usually seemed worth paying. After only three days in Nick's company certain habits, like his insistence on three meals a day, were starting to get on her nerves.

But as the evening in Lily's wore on, Celia's doubts faded. Nick was being so warm and attentive that she almost started to believe that they really were in love.

'Lily, I've got wonderful news.' Celia was up at the bar collecting another round of drinks. 'We've decided to come back in September and rent a cottage for a few months.'

'Yourself and your young man?'

'That's right. Maybe you could keep an eye open for a place for us.'

'I'll do better than that. I'd say I'll have you fixed up before you leave.'

'But we're off tomorrow afternoon.'

Lily looked at the clock. 'In half an hour now Jimmy Lordon will walk in here with the lads. He's the man you're looking for, he's some lovely houses for rent.'

'Lily, you're amazing. Thanks a million.'

'I'll send him over to you as soon as he comes in.'

Nick was sceptical about Lily's promise.

'Don't you think we should wait till tomorrow and phone an estate agent in Skibbereen?'

'What for? We're in Bally C now and Lily knows everyone. If Lily says this Jimmy Lordon is the man to see, then that's that. We'll probably get a far better deal without involving an estate agent.'

'Who is Jimmy Lordon anyway?'

'I don't know. I never knew that many people here, and the ones I did know were mostly blow-ins. He sounds like one of the lads. That's what they call the old-timers around here.'

'It seems they have a name for everyone.'

'We'll be blow-ins,' said Celia, 'unless we stay long

enough to be settlers. You soon learn the language.'

Nick smiled. 'I hadn't thought Ireland would be so different. So foreign.'

'Maybe that's just Bally C. It's a queer old place.'

'No, it's more than that. I can't really explain it. Like at the B & B this morning when that woman was talking about storing the delf' in the press – unbelievably quaint.'

'It doesn't strike me as quaint.'

'But you wouldn't use those words talking to me, would you?'

'No, because you're English. But I would to her.'

Celia in London with her cosmopolitan gloss had never struck Nick as having much of an Irish identity. It had been hidden from him because he didn't know what to look for. This had turned out to be a most extraordinary weekend in all sorts of ways. His decision to leave his wife was a sudden reprieve from a life-sentence, astounding in its simplicity. The very prospect made him feel light-headed, and added to his strange feeling that somehow everything was just a bit unreal.

Jimmy Lordon was not one of the lads, but, Celia guessed, about her own age or younger. He was compactly built with a long serious face whose haughty look contrasted with his uncombed brown hair and frayed shirt collar. Nick noticed with amusement that the man actually had bits of straw sticking out of his hair, and made a mental note to think up some joke about this rustic detail for Celia's amusement.

Despite his shabby appearance Jimmy Lordon was indeed the owner of three cottages in the Bally C area, and he described them to Nick and Celia. He spoke slowly, as if his mind were elsewhere: 'I've a terraced house in Bally C, just around the corner here. Then there's Bawnavota, that's about a mile and a half out of town, up the mountain. And I've a cottage on the edge of the sea out at Ardbeigh.'

'The edge of the sea sounds perfect,' said Celia.

'I wouldn't recommend it at that time of year,' said Jimmy. 'The last winter tenants I had there complained about the out-haul. They said they got no sleep with it in the gales.'

'What's the out-haul?' asked Nick.

'It's just a noise the tide makes when it's going out,' said Celia. 'That's why they call it Roaring Water Bay.'

Jimmy seemed impatient at this interruption, so Nick made an effort to be businesslike: 'What sort of price are you asking?'

'Oh, I wouldn't worry about that,' said Jimmy, in a way that Nick found infuriatingly vague. 'It's a long let, is it?'

'Say four months to start with.'

'We'll come to some arrangement. I must get back to the lads now. I'll pick you up at ten o'clock. Are you on?'

'Fine. Thanks a lot.'

Celia kept watching Jimmy Lordon out of the corner of her eye as he chatted to the old men up at the bar. Every so often his face was lit up by a wide, frank smile, which always lasted slightly longer than Celia expected, after which he would look down at the floor while his mouth composed itself again into a stern line. Celia thought that Jimmy Lordon was probably an extremely interesting man.

Three weeks later at six o'clock on a Thursday evening Nick and Celia met in a gloomy pub off Chancery Lane, just as they had done every Thursday for the past six months. They used that pub because it was close to both their places of work, but so unattractive that none of their colleagues ever drank there. They sat at a corner table, each with a glass of acidic white wine in front of them. Nick was looking haggard.

'I told her,' he said.

'About us?'

'Yes.'

'And Bally C?'

'Yes.'

'How did she take it?'

'Badly.'

'Oh.'

'Very badly. More or less cracked up.'

'–'

'She says I have to choose. Decent access to the kids or you and a legal battle.'

'So?'

'I won't be going to Bally C. I'm taking the kids to the seaside while she calms down.'

'–'

'Have another drink.'

'A large one.'

'So what are you going to do?' said Nick.

'Go to Bally C alone I suppose,' said Celia.

They proceeded to get drunk, each hoping to avoid a post mortem by sustaining a flippant discussion of practicalities.

'I wish I'd taken your flat while it was going,' said Nick. 'She's thrown me out.'

'I still have it for one more week.'

'I'm off with the kids tomorrow.'

'I'd been suspecting it was too good to be true. You and Bally C and no need to TEFL or worry about money . . .

'Christ! What are you going to do for money?'

'Come back when it runs out. Or get some sort of a job.'

'In Bally C? – Look, the rent at Bawnavota's paid up until Christmas, remember Jimmy gave me a special deal for payment in advance, and I can send you something when . . .'

'Oh, don't! I'll survive somehow, I've got a bit saved. If I go there alone it's because I want to. I might as well get something out of this mess.'

'Celia, I'm so sorry.'

'Shut up. Let's have another drink.'

She went back alone to her flat. She left the pub shortly before closing time while Nick was in the gents. To escape more apologies, banalities, recriminations. The aftermath of 'temporary insanity' – that being the only explanation Nick had offered for his behaviour.

'What is love,' Celia had said in a melodramatic voice, 'if not temporary insanity?'

She was at the time renting a basement which she referred to as 'the bunker' – a small dark bedroom and a small dark sitting room with the kitchen in a windowless passage that led to the windowless bathroom. Two years ago she had been delighted to find it; now she was overjoyed to be leaving it, whatever the circumstances.

The sitting room was littered with Celia's possessions, roughly sorted into three piles – stuff to sell, stuff to store with friends and stuff to take to Bally C. She picked her way through it carrying a bottle of wine and a glass and sank down on to the floor cushions (stuff to store). Her gloom lifted a little as her feet kicked a pile of books, knocking off it a set of thermal underwear, a torch and a pile of cassettes (stuff to take to Bally C).

From the very first, out on the Mizen Head, the Bally C-with-Nick project had seemed too good to be true. As so often happens, now that the worst had come, it didn't seem all that bad.

In the years since leaving Liam, Celia had not had a single affair that, in retrospect, she could call happy. She had come to expect the worst, and here it was again. But, like many people with a strong fatalistic streak, prone to mild depressions, Celia was also an optimist, ready to bounce back on a wave of enthusiasm at the slightest encouragement.

She had lost Nick and her flat. But she still had her

savings and her car, and halfway up a mountain outside Bally C was an empty house awaiting her arrival. Once again she was setting off alone on an adventure, and this time a particularly crazy one. But it meant that she was free of the bunker and its depressing darkness, free of the tedium of TEFLing, and free of London and the expectations it had disappointed. She was leaving the familiar dark corners for good.

SEPTEMBER

Celia was sitting in a bleak kitchen at the corner of a trestle table, her feet stretched out to the coal fire, waiting for Jimmy Lordon.

When Nick made the deal with him they'd arranged to pick up the keys from Lily on arrival. Celia had driven into Bally C soon after five o'clock on a Sunday and found the bar locked. There was a note pinned to the door saying 'Keys at house, see you about six. J. L.' She'd driven a mile and a half up the mountain and found the key in the latch and a fire in the grate.

It was half past five and raining steadily. Up to this point the impetus of mechanical action – clearing out, packing, storing, even the journey itself – had stopped her from thinking clearly about what she was doing. The aim had been to get to Bally C. Now that she was there, panic was starting to set in. What had previously been a whim, achieved more easily than expected, now seemed like the act of a lunatic. What the hell was she doing sitting alone in a cold damp cottage halfway up a mountain over a mile away from her nearest neighbour, with no job, not a lot of money and no close friends in the area?

The isolated stone-built cottage with its outhouses and half-acre of uncultivated land had struck Nick and Celia as a lonely place, but beautiful: ideal for two people who wanted nothing more than each other's company. It was not surprising then that she found the prospect of living there alone so daunting. Already, after half an hour, she was feeling trapped and cut off from the world outside, and was tense from listening for her landlord's car.

She was starting to feel deeply miserable when at last she heard the clatter of a diesel engine and through the window saw a rusty old Land Rover coming up the boreen.

Jimmy jumped out of the driver's door followed by two setters, one red and one white. The white dog disappeared behind the house. As Celia opened the front door the red setter jumped up and licked her face.

'Down Daisy, down,' shouted Jimmy.

Celia fondled Daisy's head. 'Come on in. Thanks for the fire, it's lovely.'

Daisy ran over and lay in front of it, her tail lashing against the hearth rug. Celia reached for the bottle of whiskey which was the only thing she'd yet brought in from the car.

'Can I offer you a drop of hot?'

'Thanks, I'll take it as it comes. It's Ben's birthday and the whole village is up there. That's why Lily's was closed.'

'Oh, I see.' That explained why Jimmy was dressed so formally compared with their previous meetings: a sports jacket and tie and faded corduroy trousers.

'Good luck.'

'Luck.'

Jimmy pulled a chair up to the table and smiled at Celia.

'So how do you like it?'

'Well, to be quite honest . . .' Celia checked herself, and wondered whether to tell Jimmy that she'd been having regrets about taking the place. Then she remembered that he also owned a terraced house in Bally C itself, and decided that there was nothing to lose by making enquiries.

'The place is fine, it's perfect. The trouble is, Nick couldn't make it, so I'll be here on my own, and I was just thinking it might be a bit much, a bit out of the way, you know. I was wondering if you'd have anywhere in the village . . .'

Jimmy slammed his glass of whiskey down on the table,

and she feared for a moment that he would be throwing her out altogether.

'The village is it? You'd rather be down below with all the bright lights and bustle?'

Bright lights and bustle in Bally C? Well, maybe in comparison with this place, she thought. He went on:

'Now isn't that a coincidence? I've only the one place in the village and I was planning on living there myself for the winter since you'd be up here. But if it suits you better to be down there, then I'd rather be up here. It's that much nearer to my horses and it's a far better place for the dogs.'

'I'd much prefer to be down in Bally C.' It was like discovering an unexpected mutual interest while chatting to a stranger on a train.

'A'course the house is much smaller, and it's not done up for visitors at all. If you'd like it' – he paused, calculating – 'you can have it till the week before Easter for the same rent you've paid me here until Christmas. If you follow me. But then I'll have to move you out so that I can do it up for the tourist season. I can get eighty pounds a week for it in the season.' He looked solemn as he said that, and replaced his empty glass slowly on the table. Celia finally realised that he was more than half-jarred, which would explain his warmth and confidentiality. On their previous meeting he had been perfectly civil, but also aloof and very controlled. It occurred to her, as she refilled his glass, that he might regret his decision in the morning, so she asked:

'Do you think we could do the swap tonight to save me unpacking twice?'

'We can a'course. Give me an hour. I'll be down there and have my gear in the Land Rover in no time. You've brought your own linen?'

'Yes.'

'Tell you what . . .' He thumped his glass on the table, spilling some of its contents. 'I took Lily and Pake home from the party. She'll be open by now. I'll meet you there in an hour. The house is only a few doors away from Lily's. Finish your drop and leave the key in the latch and I'll see you below.'

He stood up, drained his glass, and left without further formalities.

Celia stood and watched his battered Land Rover disappearing down the boreen, its back number-plate tied on crookedly with string. Only as he disappeared from sight did she remember that Daisy was still sleeping on her hearth, and the other dog still roaming in the grounds. She decided that the best thing to do was to leave them be, and get down to Lily's as soon as possible.

Lily was sitting at the bar with a cup of tea, recovering from an unaccustomed indulgence in sweet sherry at Ben's fiftieth birthday party. She stood up to welcome Celia and apologise for her earlier absence, then went behind the bar to pull a pint of lager.

'That's on the house, my dear,' she said. 'Welcome back. And where's the nice young man that's staying with you?'

'London,' said Celia, with a finality that deterred Lily from further questions. 'I've done a swap with Jimmy. He's going up the mountain and I'll be taking his house down here.'

'Old Mrs Beatty's place? Now isn't that great. You'll be just around the corner.'

The front door swung open and a tall woman in a checked shirt walked in, followed by a shorter one with a gypsy scarf tied around her hair, a baby on her hip and a toddler at her knees. They were followed by two almost toothless young men, a giggling young couple, and more children. Celia quickly identified this invasion as the remnants of Ben's birthday party. She was squashed into a corner on her bar stool and ignored, as the invasion grew bigger and louder.

When Lily's was quiet people usually sat up at the bar on tall, shabbily upholstered stools, coveted seats known as the front bench. Opposite the front bench was the wooden shop counter. It was many years since the shop counter had seen a coat of paint, and its wooden top had been worn smooth by its secondary function as extra seating on busy nights. There were two tables with low stools at either end of the bar, one next to the front door and the other beside the door to the large back room. Lily had long ago given up the privilege of keeping the back room as her own private sitting room, and it was now used as a TV room and a general extension. In winter, she lit a fire in the grate, to make it welcoming. There were some old tables of different heights and sizes and an ill-matched assortment of hard-backed kitchen chairs.

The ladies' toilet was at the top of a small staircase off the TV room, and as Celia made her way towards it she had to step over at least a dozen children who were sitting on the floor clutching bottles of red lemonade and packets of crisps and watching a Walt Disney programme. A small boy, maybe eight or nine years old, with a long blond fringe turned to Celia and said 'Hello' in a solemn voice.

'Hi.'

'My name is Edward.' He stuttered slightly.

'I'm Celia.'

'Celia, you're breaking my heart!' sang a slightly bigger red-haired boy. Much mirth ensued among the infants. Celia ignored them and climbed the steps to the ladies blushing in anger. Horrible brats.

Fortunately for their welfare, the children were all absorbed in the TV programme on her return, all except Edward. He was standing at the foot of the stairs waiting for her.

'Tttttell me,' he said, 'Do you like the Wonderful World of Disney?'

'No.'

She walked past him and back into the crowded bar. Still no sign of Jimmy and someone was sitting on her bar stool. She started to hate this loud self-possessed crowd of people milling around in their shabby-exotic clothes as if they owned the place, and laughing with each other at incomprehensible jokes:

'And then he said my name is Boris and I am not a Nazi.'

Roars of laughter.

'I am not even German, I am from Middelburg. Middelburg is a Dutch town in Holland.'

Shrieks.

'So he took them back to *Château Despair*.'

Howls.

'He knows as much about purebreds as I know about wheelbarrows.'

HA HA HA

She pushed her way through the crowd towards her bar stool beside the front door and saw that the person leaning an arse on it was Clarissa. She reached across Clarissa for her pint.

'Welcome back,' Clarissa said. 'Lily tells me I've taken your seat.'

'Go ahead, I'm just waiting for Jimmy.'

'Where's the lovely Nick?'

'London.' He was in fact still on the Isle of Wight with his children, but Celia did not want to go into details. It all seemed irrelevant, as if she'd split up with Nick a long time ago.

'So what happened, you bust up?'

'Yes.'

'Married, uh?' Clarissa laughed.

Celia nodded.

'How old are you?' Clarissa was very far gone.

'Thirty-three.'

'Whew!' Clarissa blew out a cloud of cigarette smoke.

'Thirty bloody three and you still haven't learnt. Married

men never leave their home comforts when it comes to the crunch. Never. Biggest bloody shits around, I'm telling you . . . fine for the occasional fuck if you like that sort of thing, otherwise forget it!'

'Where's Ben?'

'Passed out.' Clarissa looked well on her way to joining him as she groped on the bar for her glass. 'Finished all the booze and passed out. His idea of a good party.'

Celia looked at her watch as Clarissa continued in her booming voice. 'Are you aware of the incidence of alcoholism among the consorts of alcoholic writers?'

(O Lord deliver me. Where the hell is Jimmy?)

'A pint of lager, please, Lily. Clarissa?' Impossible not to offer a drink.

'A large glass of whiskey.'

Lily looked at Clarissa and poured a glass of lager.

'I asked for a large whiskey!'

'And you're lucky to get a glass of lager. The state of you!' Lily took the money from Celia and moved up the bar, her mouth set in a hard line.

Clarissa turned her attention to a tall woman with short sandy hair who was standing beside her, then pulled at Celia's sleeve.

'Celia, you have to meet Emily.'

Emily, the tall woman, gave a military-style salute and staggered slightly.

'I'm pissed,' she said.

'Most unusual for the General,' said Clarissa. 'That's what we call our Emily, the General. Most efficient, our Emily, she'll organise the arse off you. The General doesn't hardly never get pissed!'

'Hardly ever,' said the General loudly, then she put her arm around Clarissa's shoulder and bent her head to whisper something in Clarissa's ear.

Celia backed away and stood self-consciously between two loud groups in the middle of the bar sipping her lager, until Jimmy's face in the door rescued her from what had become a hell-hole.

Celia knew that the house was right for her the moment that she stepped into its tiny entrance hall and stared at an ornate holy water font hanging on the wall above a plant stand.

It was situated up a side street at right angles to the main road and Lily's. From the outside it was a perfectly symmetrical two-storey cottage on the end of a terrace – a window on either side of the front door and three windows above. It was painted pale green and a spiral of smoke rose from the chimney at its gable end.

There were two doors off the front hall: the one on the right led to a tiny, over-furnished parlour which Celia knew she would never use. The left-hand room was also small, but more practical. A modern wood-burning stove standing on a tiled platform dominated one side of it. There were two fireside chairs, and opposite the stove was an immense built-in dresser on which sat an old TV set. There was a square formica table with four kitchen chairs in front of the window. Apart from the faded green and beige lino and the beige fireside chairs everything was either pink or turquoise – turquoise formica on the table-top, turquoise dresser and turquoise walls, pink curtains, pink shelves to the left of the stove and pink plastic seats on the kitchen chairs. An everlasting candle glowed on a small shelf in front of a large framed picture of the Sacred Heart. Looking up at the ceiling Celia noticed a four-bar wooden railing for the drying of clothes, something she had not seen since her childhood, when a similar contraption had adorned the kitchen ceiling in Ballsbridge.

Opposite the window was a door to the kitchen which was in fact part of a long narrow extension that had been built on for Mrs Beatty quite recently. It was, to Celia, disappointingly modern, with its stainless steel sink and electric cooker. Jimmy showed her a half-bottle of milk in the fridge and the tea caddy. A door on the left gave access to the fuel store and thence the street, and on the right was a starkly functional bathroom running with condensation.

'I'll give you a tip,' said Jimmy, when a clammy dampness hit them on opening the bathroom door. 'What I do on bath night is I leave the kitchen door closed and the bathroom door open and leave the oven on full blast for half an hour with the oven door open. Heats it up like a sauna.'

'It is a bit damp, isn't it?'

'It's the Hartes next door. They've trouble with the drains and there's nothing I can do until they decide to fix it.'

They continued their tour by climbing up the staircase whose first three steps were visible at the back of the sitting room. The narrow steps then twisted around behind a plywood partition and emerged on a minuscule landing. Halfway up the stairs was a sash window whose base was level with the floor. Jimmy pulled it open to show Celia the flat roof above the kitchen extension, overlooking the terrace's communal back garden and, beyond, the broad sweep of the foothills of Mount Cornelia.

'Great little sun trap,' he said. 'There's a washing line out there too.'

'Beautiful view!' It was still daylight, but from the west-facing window Celia could see the red sun setting behind the mountains, its rays penetrating the dark grey clouds and creating multiple silver linings.

There were three tiny bedrooms, the biggest one dominated by a small double bed.

'That's where I was sleeping so it's well aired.'

Celia decided she would sleep there too.

After a short course of instruction on the eccentricities of the wood burner, Jimmy took his leave. Celia fetched her car from the main street and parked it outside her front door. The task of unpacking, which she had dreaded, was effortlessly achieved, and an hour later she was sitting at the formica table looking around in satisfaction at the evidence of her occupation – a bottle of whiskey and her radio-cassette player on top of the dresser, her poetry books on one bookshelf and a dozen paperbacks on the other. Jimmy had left a rich smell of wet dog and horse tack in the house which mingled not unpleasantly with wood-smoke from the stove. Celia breathed it in deeply and liked it.

She could hear the crowd leaving Lily's at early Sunday closing, jocular shouts, car engines starting up, then suddenly silence.

It was just as well that Celia had always enjoyed her own company, because she was alone for most of the time during her first weeks in Bally C.

She allowed herself to relax, and adapt to the slower pace of life. It was the feeling of unwinding that one experiences on a good holiday, and Celia was pleased that this was not merely a holiday, but a permanent change.

She was quick to appreciate certain aspects of Bally C: its compactness, the familiar faces in its streets and shops, the old-fashioned courtesy retained in commercial transactions – exchanges about the weather at the cash desk of the self-service grocer (always referred to as 'the supermarket' in much the same spirit as the hotel was called the Hilton), the polite 'hallo' from the bank teller which preceded the cashing of a cheque, the way that the butcher wrapped her small purchases in brown paper and string.

Then there was the simple pleasure of living in the mountains and close to the sea. Every time she looked out of her staircase window at the bleak, mainly uninhabited landscape she felt a sense of relief and exhilaration. But she regretted not having a view of the sea from her cottage.

There were several beautiful coastal walks that she knew of, and every day she intended to set off on one, but a deep lethargy, which she later thought of as a state of shock, prevented her from doing anything beyond the small tasks necessary for survival.

Celia had never lived in the country before, and it was over six years since she'd spent more than a long weekend in Ireland. She was surprised not to feel the urge to rush off to other parts of the country and visit friends. She attributed her inertia to laziness, and justified it by the price of petrol. Cork city was over two hours' drive away, and Dublin was at least five. She had never liked Dublin, finding it claustrophobically small and provincial, which was why she had left it at the first opportunity. But, ironically, in Bally C, which was genuinely small and provincial, there was none of the claustrophobia she'd always felt in Dublin. Bally C was first and foremost an experience of living in the country: that it also happened to be in Ireland was, to Celia, a very unimportant consideration.

She was living on a fixed sum of money per week, and soon realised that in order to survive she would have to limit her visits to Lily's quite strictly – Friday night, Sunday lunchtime and one other evening. Ben and Clarissa were on a similarly strict regime, imposed by Clarissa in the interests of Ben's health, which limited their daily presence in Lily's to the hours between five and seven, as well, of course, as Sunday lunchtime. The short Sunday lunch opening was as popular in Lily's as in any bar.

Celia usually started her visits to Lily's by attaching herself to Ben and Clarissa. Ben, much to her surprise, seemed to take a great interest in her life, and went to much trouble to ensure that she was introduced to the people around him and included in their conversations. When alone he and Clarissa filled her in on the gossip surrounding her new acquaintances.

Celia's travels had left her with a strong but not infallible instinct for picking out new people who were likely to become friends. The first time she saw Emily again, in her familiar red-checked shirt, she decided that Emily was not her type. Emily's tall masculine physique and short hair made Celia suspect that Emily might be bi-sexual. Emily seemed to have no memory of their previous meeting, but spent a good ten minutes with Clarissa reconstructing the events of the evening of Ben's birthday party with horrified shrieks that seemed adolescent, if not plain childish to Celia:

– I must have been *langers* –

– I was totally *smashed* –

– I can't remember a *thing* –

– Just as well –

– Oh my God, was it *that* bad? –

Emily only appeared at Sunday lunchtime, and was always accompanied by her two children. Edward, the younger child, was the solemn stuttering nine-year-old who had greeted Celia so courteously with a question about the World of Disney on the night of her arrival in Lily's.

From Ben Celia learnt that Emily's husband had gone back to London about four years ago leaving Emily with the children, a dairy herd and a market garden, all of which she looked after with very little outside help. She had also managed to get her cheeses on to the cheeseboards of Ireland's best restaurants and her vegetables were in demand by caterers as far afield as Limerick, Cork City and Kinsale. Celia tended to agree with Clarissa who complained that she found Emily's competence daunting, and continued to feel uneasy in her presence.

Ian was more approachable, a jaunty Cockney in his late twenties with one gold ear-ring and a spotted bandeau tied around his shoulder-length hair. At first sight Celia recoiled from his appearance, thinking him to be some drug-damaged relic of the hippie era. A few minutes' polite conversation with Ian was enough to correct that impression and make Celia decide to get to know him better. His straightforward cheerfulness and enthusiasm were a welcome change from Clarissa's habitual sarcasm.

Celia had arrived at the tail-end of the holiday season, and quickly learnt to distinguish between visitors, or 'strangers' as they were called, and settlers. It seemed that an inverted snobbery operated among the settlers. Wealthy city people were tolerated more than welcomed, and the minute they left the bar Ben or Ian would start mimicking their accents and attitudes. Impecunious hitch-hikers and young French and Dutch visitors were more likely to be included in a friendly conversation and encouraged to talk about themselves. But with these people Celia was aware of a dilettante attitude emanating from Ben and Clarissa which seemed to dictate that a stranger could only be interesting for so long. They would often drop someone as suddenly as they had taken him or her up and go into an exclusive huddle with other residents over a game of cards or a piece of local news.

It seemed rather arrogant to Celia at first but she soon discovered that she too preferred the continuity of regular contact with a very small group of people to the bantering exchange of life histories that went on with the strangers. It embarrassed her each time she was faced with the inevitable question of what she was doing in Bally C. The honest answer – I don't know – was usually taken as an evasive joke, which turned into a ludicrous guessing game: writer? artist? tax exile? – until someone came to her rescue by changing the subject.

As September drew to a close the trickle of visitors ceased and Celia was left alone with the hard core of Lily's clientele. Jimmy sometimes appeared, but only greeted her with a nod from the distance and stayed up at the far end of the bar with the old-timers.

'Stuck-up little bastard,' said Clarissa one evening while smiling a greeting to Jimmy from her corner of the bar.

'Who? Jimmy?'

'Yeah,' said Ben. 'The half-sir we call him. One minute he's acting like he's your best friend in the world and next thing he won't even give you the time of day. Blows hot and cold. Mostly cold.'

'I wouldn't trust him as far as I could throw him,' said Clarissa. 'Have you seen him poncing around on his horse yet?'

'It's a beautiful animal,' said Celia.

Jimmy's unsociability did not worry her. She was more than happy with the rest of the company. Besides Ben, Clarissa, Emily and Ian, there were various Macarthys, an apparently vast collection of brothers and sisters referred to by Ben as the Clan Macarthy. Celia had heard of the Macarthys years ago when visiting Bally C with Liam, but only now did she start to meet them. They were the children of the local GP who'd died some ten years ago, six months after his wife. Seven children were orphaned. The eldest Macarthy, Daniel, was only twenty at the time, but had insisted in doing everything possible to keep the family together in their home, Dromderrig House. Now the youngest Macarthy was sixteen, and although not all of them lived permanently in Bally C, they were all regular visitors. Clarissa said you could always tell a Macarthy by the teeth, or rather the lack of them. Celia discovered this was not strictly accurate. It was only Daniel and Charlie, the two eldest brothers, who lacked most of their front teeth. Daniel was dark and thickset and Charlie was fair and tall so she used the teeth to remind herself that they were brothers. They also had the same raucous laugh – a high-pitched giggle – and it was by the laugh that she came to identify the other Macarthys.

Then there was Boris, a mournful-looking Dutchman with a walrus moustache. His first words to Celia, before they had been introduced, were, 'Do you knit?' He was disappointed to hear that she did not, then startled her by remarking that he was not a Nazi and neither was he German. Her polite interest was rewarded by a lengthy description of his home town, Middelburg, and a lesson in the history and geography of Holland which bored her stiff.

Ben later explained that Boris had once been beaten up in a bar in Tralee following a misunderstanding about his nationality and his political affiliations, and had therefore adopted this standard form of self-introduction. Watching Boris make himself known to strangers in Lily's was a spectacle much enjoyed by the regulars. Boris exported handmade knitwear, and the rattle of knitting needles was a familiar sound in Bally C. Some long-established convention ruled that in Lily's only Lily was allowed to knit. Other people delivered socks and sweaters to Boris on Friday evenings in Lily's back room, picking up cash payments and next week's wool. Celia noticed with admiration that Ian was producing two pairs of socks a week, and wondered whether, if it came down to it, he would teach her the craft.

Celia was glad that Jimmy had left the old black and white television on top of the dresser in her house. She bought the RTE Guide every week and encircled with red biro the programmes that she intended to watch. There were not many of these.

Once a week she drove into Skibbereen, usually on a Friday afternoon, on the pretext of shopping for odd things that she could not find in Bally C. The real reason was to have an outing to break the routine.

By the third week the lack of activity involved in her routine began to worry her. She got up late and began to tackle the first chore – the lighting of the stove – while drinking her first cup of coffee. Once it had caught – often as late as 2.30 – she was able to go out to the shops and buy food. Then she would sit at the formica-topped table drinking cups of coffee and looking out of the window until it was time for Lily's or the television or her evening meal. Sometimes she dipped into the poetry books that she had brought with her – Chaucer, Keats, Hardy and others that she had enjoyed at university, which always accompanied her on travels. But most of all she liked to look out of her window. Nothing dramatic ever happened out there, but for the moment she needed no more to amuse her than the possibilities offered by this small view.

The window gave directly on to the road with no intervening pavement. On the other side of the road was a grey stone bank about six feet high, and above it, behind a big tangle of bramble bushes, a field. Sometimes there were cows in the field. The cows often leant over the edge of the steep bank, poking their heads and forefeet through gaps in the brambles to eat the grass that grew on top of the stone wall. It got quite exciting wondering whether one of the cows would fall off.

To the right of the window, also on the opposite side of the road, was a telegraph pole, and on the left was an alcove in the stone bank housing a water tap. People came and filled buckets and plastic jerry cans at the tap to take water to their beasts. The only one she knew by name as yet was Ian. There was one old man who always put the galvanised bucket on an empty sack on the roof of his station wagon before driving off down the road. Sometimes Celia got up and stood at the front door to watch him drive the 300 yards to his herd. The bucket had never yet fallen off, but the prospect that it might was almost as exciting as that of the cows who might one day fall off the bank.

Sometimes Jimmy Lordon rode by, crouched on the back of a chestnut mare with a jockey's crash helmet on his head. Sometimes another man, also crash-helmeted, rode by with him on a big grey.

Then there were the neighbours. She saw only old women, but judging by the washing that they hung up on the bushes and lines in the communal back garden, there were men in the terrace too. In time she learnt to distinguish three of the women, which she considered to be quite an achievement. They were all very short, and stout. They all wore nylon overalls and ankle socks and carried brightly coloured plastic bowls full of washing. They had to pass her window to gain access to the terrace garden, and seeing her sitting there, day after day, they got into the habit of giving her a neighbourly wave which she returned. She was impressed because they were all perfectly hideous. Of the three whom she 'knew' one had a straggling white beard, one (who always smiled broadly) had no teeth and the third had matted grey hair which stood up in short peaks, and wild rolling eyes.

OCTOBER

For an hour and a half Celia had been trying to light the fire, faithfully following Jimmy's instructions. The hour and a half was not unusual, but today it started to worry her. The glowing coals kept ticking. Surely fires shouldn't tick? Then the tick turned into a flame which broke out from the bottom of the little pile of coals and licked its way to the top. Triumph! Almost time to break the heap of coals with the poker and put more little pieces on top of the glowing ones, until she had enough coals blazing to allow her to shove a couple of big logs on top, close the stove door, and forget about it until evening.

She prodded the pile of coals gently with the poker. The precarious structure collapsed leaving only one glowing ember. Quietly, without swearing, she broke off another bit of firelighter, lit it, and piled more coals on top of it.

Stupid way to get a wood burner going, she thought to herself, this morning as every morning. Kindling and newspapers, that's what I need. Loads of *Examiners* out the back, but no kindling. She had tried to buy kindling in Skibbereen, but the fuel merchant had shaken his head saying that there was no call for it.

She was sure that other people used kindling, and wondered yet again where they got it from. Then she had an idea.

Every day, she decided, she would go for a walk with two big strong plastic bags. In the course of her walk she would fill the bags with sticks and twigs and dry them out in her fuel store until she had accumulated a decent supply of kindling. That would solve two problems at once: an end to the hellish daily chore of getting the stove going, and the disappearance of some of the extra flesh which had formed on her hips since arriving in Bally C.

Gumboots. Unpretentious black gumboots. Purchased Skibbereen circa 1973. Yellow oilskin jacket of local manufacture. Birthday present with matching yellow oilskin trousers from mother-in-law circa 1975. Woolly bobble hat acquired along with other odd bargains in a Kenmare emporium long ago. In the early days. 1969? Liam had a matching one, or this was perhaps originally Liam's and he now had hers. More likely he had lost it or given it away.

Blast.

Celia stood in the hallway of her house stuffing plastic bags into the pockets of her yellow jacket and trying not to feel self-conscious about the amount of protective clothing that she found necessary to put on for this walk. It was not raining, but it looked as if it might. It had rained yesterday so anywhere off the road would be muddy, and she reckoned she was unlikely to find many sticks without leaving the road. Cipíní, she and Liam used to call them, those Christmasses . . .

Blast.

She was spending ever more time fighting off memories of Liam, whom she had scarcely thought about since leaving Ireland. Now, back in Bally C, the memories came surging up with startling clarity at the slightest provocation. The worst thing about it was that they were all happy memories of the nice times, the times they had shared before things started going wrong.

When she was not fighting off memories of Liam she was worrying about what on earth she was doing, or rather, not doing. She never went out except to shop or visit Lily's. She was not, as various strangers in Lily's had assumed, writing. Nor was she painting. Both occupations would have been considered unremarkable in Bally C, but she had neither the talent nor the inclination to take them up. She had no plans to start farming or gardening or potting, nor to look for a part-time bar-maid job as Ben had suggested. He had even remarked that she *looked* like a good bar-maid, and when she said 'You mean because I'm fat and jolly' and he said 'Yes' they very nearly had their first tiff. Celia used to worry a lot about her size before she had acquired a lack of occupation to worry about as well. Collecting kindlings was not all lucrative, but at least it was something to do.

Here goes, she thought, as she opened the front door. One overdressed fat woman in search of cipíní. She looked right and left, then slammed the front door behind her (it tended to stick if she didn't) and walked up the road away from the village looking, she hoped, purposeful.

There were several new bungalows on the road out of Bally C, one of which had the local undertaker's hearse parked beside it. She had deliberately chosen not to take the road past the bungalow which had belonged to her in-laws.

She passed Ian's caravan next. It was neatly fenced in by chicken wire which formed a compound for Ian's two goats, evil-looking creatures. She noticed a hand-painted wooden sign tacked on to the gatepost saying *Château Despair* and she decided that Ian was probably even more interesting than she thought.

Celia relaxed once she was past Ian's place, and began to pick up a good rhythm. There was no need to stop as there was not a stick in sight. The hedges consisted mainly of banks on which long grass and cow parsley were growing. There were also clumps of ferns which were now dying down and starting to stand out as rust-coloured patches against the greenness of the rest.

The road she had chosen ran inland, and after a couple of miles a turning to the right climbed over a small hill and led back to Bally C along the coast. Celia remembered a few wooded patches on the inland side of the hill, and this was where she expected to find her kindling.

She was sweating and slightly out of breath by the time she arrived at the first likely spot. It was a ruined cottage with the remains of an orchard beside it. She climbed over the metal gate and sat on a boulder to rest.

The last time she'd been here was the Christmas before the summer that she and Liam split up.

Blast.

No; not blast.

That was the Christmas when she had made turkey pasties for Liam and he'd taken the car off for the day on the pretext of going to Kerry to make sketches for some project. Next day she'd noticed only five miles on the clock, and no petrol gone. Under hysterical interrogation Liam admitted to spending the day with a married neighbour, Hazel, while her husband was up in Cork. Screwing, and picnicking in bed on Celia's pasties. That hurt more than the sexual infidelity; the idea of tarty old Hazel eating *her* pasties.

To hell with memories of nice sweet Liam: now she had recaptured the Liam she had left – an uncaring, promiscuous bastard.

Pasties!

Celia was an excellent cook.

She had not made pasties since that long ago day.

A Plan!

Celia dropped the kindling inside her front door and hurried on down to Lily's. As she'd expected, Lily was alone. They sat by the fire in the back room and Celia explained her plan. Lily responded with a simple phrase that lifted Celia's spirits to the sky:

'I can a'course.'

* * *

Celia's pasties – leek and potato in cheese sauce for the many vegetarians in the area, and minced lamb and potato for the rest – caught on fast in Lily's. Within a week Celia was approached by the landlord of the Penny Farthing, and his sales were three times as big as Lily's. She took a few samples into Skibbereen's delicatessen and they were soon shifting three dozen a week, mince and potato only, and two large bowls of chicken liver pâté.

Emily's finances only allowed her to visit Lily's once a week, and she chose Sunday lunchtime in order to reward herself for something which she thought of as the most disagreeable chore of the week: taking Aoife and Edward to Sunday Mass.

They had been baptised at the insistence of Emily's mother-in-law. David, their father, was indifferent to the whole business and could not understand Emily's indignation at the interference. She and David never went near the church in Bally C if they could help it. But then, two years after David's departure, Aoife had made her first communion along with other children of her age in the parish, and, ever since that time, she and Edward had forced Emily to take them down the mountain to twelve o'clock mass every Sunday and to the eight thirty on Holy Days of Obligation. And, instead of letting her go off for a cup of tea with friends while they did their religious duty, they insisted that she stay with them for the whole ceremony and stand and sit and kneel when everyone else did. She drew the line at pronouncing the responses, even after a particularly bad-tempered sermon from the parish priest himself on the topic of the discourtesy paid to God by non-responders and mutterers. If she wasn't there with them, Aoife said, their friends would call her a heathen. It was bad enough for Aoife and Edward having to explain why their father had gone off to London, without having to explain away a heathen mother too, so Emily did her bit, and tried her best not to listen to the rambling narrow-minded sermons which so infuriated her, nor to watch her children's docile piety.

After Mass they dropped into the supermarket (which was also the newsagents) where each picked up their weekly treat – the *Beano* for Edward, *Jackie* for Aoife and the *Sunday Telegraph* for Emily. About one week in three her paper did not succeed in negotiating the intricate network which existed to get it to Bally C, and on those Sundays further compensation was called for in terms of two gin and tonics at Lily's instead of her usual two beers.

On this particular Sunday there were no newspapers at all, not even Irish ones, and no explanations either.

'Two bottles of red lemonade, two packets of crisps and a gin and tonic please Lily.'

'No papers, uh?' said Ben.

'Bloody typical,' said Emily.

'Load of crap papers, who needs them?' said Clarissa.

Emily ignored her. Over the years she had had every single argument of the many it was possible to have with Clarissa and had decided to stop bothering.

'But you write for them,' said Celia.

'That's different. It's only poetry reviews and I need the money. So do the poets I review.'

'Don't expect Clarissa to be logical,' said Emily.

'You've met Celia, haven't you?' asked Ben.

'I have a'course,' said Emily. 'You make the pasties.'

Celia smiled. She liked her new identity and she was getting used to Emily. Her butchness no longer worried Celia, but seemed appropriate in a woman who ran her own smallholding with such independence and confidence.

'I wish I'd thought of it,' Emily continued. 'How's it going?'

'Fine. They're selling really. It's just a bit of a headache getting hold of good veg. Leeks especially, but even the potatoes are half rotten.'

'It's the plastic bags,' said Emily. 'They pack them when they're wet. Ignorant pigs. Where are you getting them?'

'Skibbereen.'

'And the leeks?'

'Yes.'

'That's crazy! I can give you leeks, far cheaper if you pull them yourself.'

'Can I really –'

'But a'course. I'd rather have the cash than the leeks. And you should get your spuds from Con. I only set enough for myself this year because I needed the space for veg. Con has the best potatoes in West Cork, I always get my seed potatoes from him.'

'Who is he?'

'The old-timer on the bar stool in the corner,' said Ben in a low voice. 'You'll have to watch yourself out at Con's place, he'll be asking you to stay for a bit of court. You know what that is?'

'A bit of court? You mean courting?' Celia had not heard that expression for years.

'In other words he'll try to find out if you fuck,' said Clarissa.

'Balls,' said Emily to Celia. 'He's a sweetie, there's no harm in him at all. Come on over and I'll introduce you.'

'You were lucky there,' said Ben after Emily and the children had left.

'Oh yes, it'll be great to have a regular supply of decent leeks.'

'No, I meant the spuds. Con won't sell to just anyone.'

'Why not?'

'Don't know. It's his prerogative I suppose. We used to buy spuds from him, then last week Clarissa went up and he turned around and said he had no more to sell us. Not that he had no more you notice, but he had no more to sell *us*.'

Celia nodded and Ben went on, 'I thought you'd have met

him by now. He's thick as thieves with the half-sir.'

'Jimmy?'

'Yeah. He stables his horses up near Con's place.'

'Where is he today?' Celia looked around the thinning crowd that lingered in Lily's at closing time.

'The half-sir? He comes and goes. I'd imagine he's up in Cork. He has some business racket up there.'

'Oh.' This did not fit in with Celia's impression of Jimmy as an uncomplicated sportsman who lived for his dogs and his horses. The idea that he also had to earn a living had never occurred to her.

'How do you get on with him?' asked Clarissa.

'All right. I hardly ever see him because the rent was paid in advance.'

Clarissa laughed. 'Oh yes, one of his little "special offers". You know why he does that?'

'It seemed a good deal.'

'It's so that you won't go moving out or holding back money when he doesn't do the repairs. He's a crafty operator, the half-sir.'

'Smug little bastard,' said Ben.

'Just because he doesn't get pissed every day,' said Clarissa.

'Asked me to moderate my language last week. Get him – "moderate your language please, it's upsetting my friends" –' Ben gave a perfect imitation of Jimmy's Cork city accent, an accent which always sounded prissy to ears accustomed to the broader West Cork.

'I never knew he cared about language,' said Clarissa.

'He doesn't give a fuck about language,' said Ben. 'He uses more of it than most – he was trying to get at me.'

'Oh, we're being paranoid now are we? I thought that was last year's thing.'

'Wasn't it nice of Emily to offer me the leeks,' said Celia to the glowering couple.

'She's ripping you off. She planted too many and she

can't unload them on anyone,' said Clarissa.

'Jesus wept!' said Ben. 'Can't you find anything pleasant to say about anyone today? Sometimes you really piss me off . . .'

Celia slipped away unnoticed.

Celia pulled her car in towards the ditch and looked again at the directions to Con's place that Emily had scribbled on the back of a brown envelope:

Ardbeigh road out of Bally C
Right at creamery
mile. Past pink house
First right. 1 mile-ish
Boreen l.h.s.
Past stables and first farmhouse to yellow house
If n/r hoot

She had negotiated her way successfully as far as the first right and one mile-ish stage, but there was no sign of the boreen. She made a mental note of the figure on her mileometer and started slowly up the road again.

Two miles further and there was still no sign of a boreen l.h.s. Celia turned the car around in a gateway and went slowly back down the road. It had been raining heavily all week, but today it was dry and bitterly cold for late October.

A boreen. A large bush almost hid it from view on the other approach. It was exceptionally narrow, even for that part of the country, and its banks towered above Celia's hatchback.

The boreen was unpaved, and within a few yards Celia became aware that she was in danger of getting stuck. There would probably be a paved patch for turning at the house, and if she could get that far without stopping she thought she'd be all right.

The lane made a right-angled bend then carried on downhill for about half a mile. Through her dirty windscreen Celia could see something blocking the road – an old Land Rover, its back numberplate tied on with string. She braked and felt her wheels sink into the mud.

Jimmy's Land Rover was parked across the entrance to a yard and derelict farmhouse. Celia picked up her gumboots from the floor in front of the passenger seat and opened her door to put them on. The thick red mud came up over her ankles. She walked along the narrow grass verge and into the yard.

There were loose boxes around three sides of the yard, a short distance from the dilapidated house which occupied the fourth side of the square. One loose-box door was open and banging gently against the wall. She peered into another open half-door at a chestnut rump and smiled as she heard the sound of munching hay coming from the front end of the animal. It was a long time since Celia had been near horses and the familiar sounds and smells took her straight back to childhood and the years when she'd been horse-mad.

The other loose boxes were bolted shut, and there was no sign of anyone around. The keys had been left in the Land Rover. Celia assumed that Jimmy couldn't get out without first moving her car so she left the keys in hers as well and decided to walk up on to Con's. It couldn't be far, and Jimmy would guess where to find her.

Con's house looked like an exact replica of her own, square and symmetrical, except that it was detached and built in a sheltered hollow. In so secluded a spot there was no need for net curtains, and as she passed the front window Celia saw Con sitting in a fireside chair reading the paper. She tapped on the glass and he stood up, startled.

'I didn't hear you coming at all,' he said as he opened the front door.

She paused, looking down at the sparkling lino, and at

her mud-caked boots. 'Maybe I'd better go round the back.'

'Yerra, pull them off there on the mat.' He was in stockinged feet himself, a pair of Boris's she noticed, and had his work clothes on: baggy pin-striped trousers and a threadbare brown sweater over a grey collarless shirt.

He always dressed up in his Sunday best to go to Lily's, dark suit, hair oil and all. She looked at his tousled black hair and noticed the amused glint in his china-blue eyes as he watched her trying to remove her boots while keeping on her socks, and she became aware that Con was a very attractive man, somewhere between forty and fifty she guessed. Ben's warning about Con's likely request for 'a bit of a court' no longer seemed so outrageous.

Celia adjusted her socks and followed Con into the front room.

'I left my car up the lane. Jimmy's Land Rover was in the way.'

'He's riding out.'

'Yes, I couldn't see him. And I think I'm stuck.'

'Yerra what harm? We'll give you an aul haul outa that. Sit ye down there.'

He went back into the entrance hall, moving stiffly, and up the flight of stairs that occupied the middle of the house. Once inside Con's place any similarity to Celia's ceased, apart from an identical portrait of the Sacred Heart on the wall with a perpetual candle and a fresh white doily on its altar.

The room was stark. An oblong painted table stood in the window with a wooden form under it and two kitchen chairs. An enormous wooden radio sat high on a pedestal to one side of the fireplace. Opposite the fire there was a hearth-rug and two fireside chairs. Otherwise the room was bare. She could see through to the kitchen at the back of the house, also spotlessly clean and tidy, with a view out on to the west face of Mount Cornelia.

Con came back with a bottle of whiskey and two glasses and put them down on the table.

'Ye'll have a drop.'

'Thank you.' Celia was flattered by this courtesy which was usually reserved for males on their first visit. Females got tea.

Con went through to the kitchen and fetched a glass jug of water. He limped slightly, and Celia wondered whether he was, like so many people in the area, suffering from arthritis.

'Grand day,' he said.

'It is.'

'We've had enough o' the rain.'

'Oh aye.' This was an expression that Celia had picked up from the settlers and God knows where they'd got it from. It was certainly not native West Cork, but it was contagious.

'Good luck.'

'Luck.'

Con threw another log on the fire and chuckled.

'So ye're going baking?'

'Oh aye, er, yes, I am.'

'Yerra grand little cook they tell me.' He pronounced it 'cooook'. Celia smiled.

'Ye'll make some man a fine wife.'

She laughed.

'I tell 'oo,' said Con with great animation, then he lapsed into silence. The log crackled. Celia sipped her whiskey, hoping that it would restore her powers of conversation. Con said something that she did not catch.

'Sorry?'

He repeated some kind of invitation, and this time she got the word 'horses'.

'Oh, yes.'

'Fetch your boots round the back then.'

She went to pick them up from the door mat, then

followed Con through the kitchen and out the back door. Two setters came up and fussed around them, followed by an ancient springer spaniel.

'Gerrawayoutathat!' shouted Con, aiming a kick at the nearest dog.

There were two loose boxes outside Con's back door, built into the side of a corrugated iron barn. He opened the nearest door and went inside. She watched him slip a head collar on the animal.

'That's a fine young mare now,' he said, as he led her out into the yard. She was certainly impressive as far as Celia could judge, a good strong bay with a white flash on her face, the slim legs of a thoroughbred and solid forequarters, but she was badly in need of grooming. Con pulled a lump of mud out of her mane and sniffed.

'She's a beauty. How old is she?'

'Rising three, rising three. I've her broken six months now. She'll give you a grand spin any day.'

'Really?' Celia wasn't sure if he was seriously offering her the chance to ride, or just talking in general terms.

'Yerrachild could ride her.'

'Really?'

'Have you done much riding yourself?'

'Oh, yes, when I was a kid. Every Saturday. And I've been out a few times since. I love horses.'

She tried to remember exactly when she had last ridden. It was either in Spain, where the brute had bolted with her, or in Richmond Park, where she had surprised herself by displaying some competence in comparison with the other people on the hack.

Con looked at her and chuckled.

'Every Saturday, eh?'

'When I was a child.'

The mare pawed the ground and tossed her head. Con walked her around in as big a circle as the yard would allow, talking to her in a low voice. Celia suddenly felt nervous.

'Do you hunt her?' she asked.

Con laughed. Had she said the wrong thing?

'Yerra I'm way too heavy for her girl. I'll show you now the feller I hunt.'

He led the mare back into her box and took off the head collar.

'What's her name?'

'Ballycashlinacosta Lady. The Lady, we call her. And this feller here is Dún Donncha – *gerrawayoutathat!*' He disappeared into the loose box and continued shouting. Celia removed herself to the far side of the yard.

'*Stand! Stand!*'

Con reappeared leading a mountain of a horse, the grey that Celia had seen pass her window. Close to, she thought that he had a mean look in his eye.

'*STAAAAAAAND! STAAAAAND!*' The horse kept on walking. Con dug his heels in and leant back. He was pulled along at an angle of forty five degrees for a few more paces.

'*STAND YAFUCKER!*' The horse stopped.

'Hold his head there a minute.' Before she had time to protest, Celia had a rope in her hand, the mountainous beast on the other end of it. He looked at her.

'Stand,' said Celia threateningly as she quaked in her boots.

Con walked around the horse's hindquarters and picked up one of its hind legs.

'He'll be shedding a shoe,' he said, taking the rope back from Celia. 'I'll see to that when Jimmy comes in.'

He led the grey back into the box, and said as he bolted the door, 'He's a contrary beast, I wouldn't put you up on him at all. But the mare, sure a child could ride her.'

Con muttered something else that Celia did not catch and walked off up the lane. She followed him, jogging along to keep pace with him, and wondered what was going to happen next. She was only catching about forty percent of his quick-fire remarks, but she was afraid that if she constantly asked him to repeat himself he'd get impatient with her.

They arrived at Jimmy's Land Rover. Con jumped in and moved it forwards a few yards.

'Give her a try now.'

Celia started the engine and her wheels spun uselessly, sending up a shower of mud.

'A'right!'

She switched off. Con climbed out of the driver's seat carrying a thick rope and slipped one end over the Land Rover's tow-hitch, and attached the other to Celia's car. Within minutes she was parked outside Con's house.

'Hey, thanks a million.'

Con, who was picking up an empty seed bag from outside his back door, ignored her.

The tidiness inside his house contrasted with the mess around its back and side: two tractors, piles of rusty farm implements, rotting pallets, bits of engine, multi-coloured fertiliser bags, a couple of tractor tyres and an old twin-tub washing machine. Con went into an out-house and beckoned Celia to follow him.

She had almost forgotten about the potatoes. Here they were, a great pile of them filling the gloom with a smell of earth.

'Is it big ones or small ones?' asked Con.

'Anything at all, I don't mind. They look terrific.'

'I've a good crop this year.' She helped Con to fill the bag from the pile which reached to the ceiling at the far side of the shed. He tied it with a piece of twine, then he laid it on its side in the back of her car.

'I'd say that'll keep you going for a week or two.'

'That's wonderful. The ones in the shops are all rotten. It's those plastic bags.'

'They pack'em when they're wet, fuckin' eejits.'

'Thanks a million, Con. You must tell me how much I owe you for that lot.'

'Yerra we'll settle up later. I'll see you in Lily's one night.'

'Are you sure?'

'Yerraway. You turn the car now and I'll give you a pull down to the road.'

Celia dreamt about horses that night.

Charlie Macarthy had invited Celia to his birthday party on Saturday. He was twenty-eight and Daniel was organising a feast to celebrate the event. Celia offered to contribute some food, but was told that a bottle of wine would be far more welcome. The Macarthys were all great cooks, and enjoyed combining their talents to create a spread. Dromderrig House had a large old-fashioned kitchen and this was where the party was to be held. Celia was curious to see the rest of the house, a substantial three-storey building dating from the early nineteenth century, but on her first visit she got no further than the kitchen and the downstairs bathroom.

She had been looking forward to the party as a change from Lily's, and was a little disappointed to see the same old faces arriving – Ben, Emily with her two children, Boris, Con, Barney Mack, Jimmy and Ian. Only Clarissa was missing. She was working, according to Ben. Fanny and Ownie Macarthy, the youngest of the family, were home from their schools in Cork for the weekend. They were a quiet pair of teenagers except when they laughed the raucous Macarthy laugh, which was not often. The only people she had not met before were Marie, the married sister and her husband, and when she did she realised that they had been among the crowd in Lily's on the night of her arrival.

The talk was all of Ownie's window. It had fallen out

earlier that evening from the third storey, narrowly missing Charlie who was tidying the yard.

'Nearly had me killed,' said Charlie. 'Fucking great sash window crashing at my feet, and when I asked him why the fuck he wants to go opening a window in October d'ya know what he says? He's trying to let a moth go free, he says. A moth for fucksake!'

Charlie repeated the story to each newcomer, laughing loudly at its conclusion, and Celia felt sorry for Ownie who sat quietly in a corner looking awkward. Charlie showed him no mercy.

'D'you think you could get the postman next time, Ownie? Lazy bollax is saying he won't come up with the letters anymore for fear of flying slates. When I see him again I'll tell him never mind the slates, look out for Ownie and his windows.'

It was not Ownie who lashed out at him eventually, but Fanny. Charlie would have got a stinging slap across the cheek had Daniel not caught her upraised hand in time. She ran from the room cursing Charlie. Ownie followed, only pausing to glare at Daniel and say, 'Now look what you've done'. Celia wondered why he blamed Daniel and not Charlie.

Daniel smoothed over the tense silence which followed their exit by refilling glasses and starting a long story about the new poitín-maker he was patronising. Fanny and Ownie reappeared in time for the food, and did not allow the incident to spoil their evening.

The meal was an extraordinary selection of dishes. It looked as if everyone had cooked whatever they felt like without consulting the others, but somehow it worked. There was pigeon pâté and lentil soup and home-made bread, rabbit curry, fish stew, chicken liver rissotto, baked potatoes and half a dozen different salads.

Celia was impressed by Daniel's efficiency. He was the one who organised the serving of the food and the clearing of the table, and he had baked the birthday cake for Charlie and iced it and decorated it with twenty-eight candles.

Marie's two-year-old helped Charlie to blow out the candles and the singing of 'Happy Birthday' was followed by 'For He's a Jolly Good Fellow' and shouts of 'SPEECH'.

Charlie got to his feet and began 'Ladies and gentlemen, I would just like to say . . . let's get this party on the road!'

There were great cheers, and Charlie produced a bag of uncleaned grass, his birthday present from Ian.

'Best Kerry Gold,' he said, and began shredding the leaves on to a sheet of paper.

Celia preferred Daniel's hot punch, and noticed that Jimmy and 'the lads' were the only other non-smokers. She had doubts about her ability to handle the combined effect of grass and poitín.

'Some party,' said a loud voice behind her. She turned around and saw Ben draining his glass of punch. 'And it's only just beginning,' he added, and laughed.

He was right. It was nearly six in the morning before people started to leave. Ben had passed out, and Emily's Edward and Aoife were fast asleep in a corner with Marie's two-year-old between them.

There'd been singing and recitations, dancing to Marie's fiddle and Con's gadget, blues guitar from Ian, jazz guitar from Ben, guitar duets from Daniel and Charlie, a tin whistle solo from Jimmy and a long and very funny ballad from Ownie. Everyone was expected to contribute something and when it came to Celia's turn she told a shaggy dog story and reckoned it had been a success by the number of loud groans that it produced. She danced with everybody and joined in all the choruses even though she could hardly hold a tune.

She drove home with a kaleidoscope of new memories running around in her head – Emily doing the can-can, Ian puffing on a monster joint, Jimmy up to his elbows in washing-up, Barney Mack singing a long and tuneless rebel song, Fanny's face pale and serious as she sang unaccompanied in Irish, Boris bellowing out the toreador's song from *Carmen* . . .

She reflected with satisfaction that there were six other Macarthys, all with birthdays to celebrate at some point in the year.

'Emily!' Clarissa stood on the steps of the bank and waved at Emily who was on the other side of the street about to get into her car.

'How's things?'

'Fine. I'm just off to Skib.'

'Mart day?'

'No, shopping.'

'Got time for a coffee?'

'Why not?'

'See you up at my place in five minutes, okay? Ben's around but the door's open so just go straight in and put on the kettle.'

Clarissa and Ben lived in a house on the edge of the cliff at the south end of Bally C. The front of the house looked out directly over the sea, while the wall of their back garden formed part of the main street. Consequently their 'front' door was at the side of the house.

Emily let herself in and flicked the switch on the electric kettle. Then she sat herself down in Ben's pine rocking chair and picked up the latest copy of *Time* magazine. Ben was an enthusiastic subscriber – back numbers of *Time, Newsweek, National Geographic, Country Life, The Field* and *Yachting Monthly* were stacked under the windows of his sitting room in individual piles. Emily often wondered what it was like to live the sort of life that left enough free time to read so many magazines. She did not even have a television in the house, in spite of constant pleas from the children, and preferred to read novels and thrillers in the few unoccupied hours that came to her on winter evenings.

Ben's house was functional and comfortable. It was old, but he had replaced the windows on the sea-facing side with narrow slats of floor-to-ceiling double glazing. The furniture was modern and the kitchen even had a dishwasher. In a city, Emily was well aware, it would be considered an average, unpretentious middle-class home, but in Bally C it seemed ostentatiously luxurious.

'Hello there.' Clarissa put two large plastic bags on the kitchen table and started transferring packages to the deep freeze.

'My God, that must have cost you a fortune,' said Emily.

'Fuck it. I'm working at the moment, can't think about food. If Ben wants fresh stuff he organises it.'

'How's it going?'

'Two hundred and eighty nine. It's getting extremely exciting. Eleven more poems and I'll have the three hundred.'

'I never understood why it has to be three hundred.'

'Nor do I any more. It just does. I hope to hell I survive.'

'How come you missed Charlie's party? It was a great crack. You weren't really working were you?'

'Sort of. I was out on the razz with a chap I met in Bantry. Far more fun than the Clan Macarthy and their dreadful sessions.'

'What's he like?' Emily was amazed at Clarissa's ability to find a supply of interesting men in the area. She herself had given up looking long ago.

'Nothing great. A wonderful body and a lousy fuck. I should have remembered that there is absolutely no connection between good-looking and good-in-bed. Anyway I got a rather interesting poem out of it. Short and brutal.'

'Aren't you terrified that Ben will find out?'

'Terrified? No. At the very worst he'd throw me out, and that could be a damn good thing in the long run.'

'You mean you'd get another poem out of it?'

'An epic,' said Clarissa.

Emily laughed, even though she found Clarissa's total dedication to her work obsessive, incomprehensible and at times contemptible. Clarissa's work, it seemed, could excuse all manner of anti-social, inconsiderate behaviour.

'Anything new that I can have a look at?' asked Emily.

Clarissa had no intention of showing Emily anything. She had to be at a very low ebb to need feedback from Emily. But she could not resist vaunting her latest adventure.

'How about a Con Leary poem?' she said.

'Con!' Emily was equal parts shocked and amused. This was the most unlikely one yet.

'Yes, Con,' Clarissa laughed. 'I don't think he'll ever get over it, you should have *seen* his face when he realised I wasn't just teasing . . . the only bugger is that he assumes I'll be on every time I go up for spuds, so I had to spin Ben a line about Con not wanting to sell to us anymore. Once was enough, quite frankly. Anyway, you needn't start feeling sorry for Ben. It looks as if he's planning his own bit of action at last. He says he fancies the fat lady.'

'The fat lady?'

'Pasties. Celia.'

'Hmm. Do you think she can handle it?'

'What do you mean?'

'She strikes me as the type who might go falling madly in love.'

'Oh, I think she'd be sensible enough. She didn't seem exactly cut up when that chap Nick gave her the push.'

'How do you know she wasn't?'

'Oh, was she?' Clarissa sounded indifferent. 'Maybe. But I don't imagine she'll fall for Ben, he's not a great romantic. My biggest worry is that Ian or Charlie might get there first.

Ben's one hell of a slow mover. I suppose I'll have to do something about it.'

'Oh God. Look, don't mess her around. She's nice.'

'A bit dim.'

'You think everyone's dim.'

'She's so *aimless*. She lacks obsession.'

'Good thing too,' said Emily, hoping that this pleasant gossip was not about to be interrupted by a sermon from Clarissa on the importance of total dedication to literature.

As it happened, further gossip was prevented by the entrance of Ben who had been cleaning his gun in the utility room.

'First of November tomorrow and there won't be a cock pheasant safe in the sky,' he announced, as he held out a mug for hot coffee.

NOVEMBER

Bally C was closing in on Celia and she liked it. She could now recognise people by their cars – Ben and Clarissa's bright green Volkswagen, Boris's Mercedes, Emily's Morris estate, Ian's blue van, the Macarthys' 2CV – and she enjoyed returning their friendly headlamp flashes as she drove to and from Skibbereen with her pasties. She now saluted all other traffic that she met as a matter of course by raising her hand from the steering wheel, but flashing headlamps as friends gave her a childish feeling of self-importance.

Her own smart red hatchback had long ago acquired the coating of mud which distinguished Bally C vehicles from those of strangers. It was also acquiring some of the makeshift touches which were a feature of many local cars. The lock on the rear door was playing up, and she needed to order a replacement from Cork. Meanwhile Ian had rigged up a simple system involving a loop of rope tied over the bumper and a jamming knot on the boot handle which worked perfectly well. It meant that Celia could no longer lock her car, but even Boris, who had an expensive cassette player and a big selection of tapes in the Merc, never bothered to lock his car during the quiet months. There was no crime in Bally C in the winter.

She was gradually getting to know her neighbours. One morning the woman with no teeth knocked at her door carrying a steaming pan of water. She was not only toothless, but also had a cleft palate and it was mainly by sign language that she made Celia understand that there was a power cut and that knowing that her house was all-electric, Mrs Harte had brought her the pan to leave on top of the wood burner in case she wanted a cup of tea. Celia had the good manners to invite her neighbour in at once for tea and biscuits and after half an hour she could understand the women well enough to establish a warm rapport.

It was Mrs Harte who introduced her to Con Leary's sister Peg who lived at the far end of the terrace. She was small and neat with tightly permed grey hair. Celia had never seen her before as Peg Leary had access to the back of the terrace at her own end of it. Con's sister went up to clean for him twice a week and take him his baking, and on Sundays Con came down to her with Barney Mack for lunch. Con and Barney Mack got into the habit of walking back there from Lily's in Celia's company, and waiting to see her in her front door.

Celia was first introduced to Barney Mack in Lily's on one of the many occasions when she tried to settle up with Con for her sack of potatoes. Barney Mack was a real old-timer, bent double by arthritis and racked by a rolling bronchial cough. He was the man whom she had often watched in her early weeks in Bally C as he drove up the road to his herd with a galvanised bucket on the roof of his estate car. Celia did not like Barney Mack. He was gruff to the point of rudeness and so often ignored her friendly greetings that she stopped saluting him altogether.

The mist came down while Celia was lighting the fire – a task she accomplished nowadays in about five minutes, with the help of the kindling.

It was the first Saturday in November and she had no need to cook pasties until Sunday. She had planned a trip to Bantry with Ian and Charlie for the afternoon showing of a Monty Python film.

The mist was so thick that she could not even see the telegraph pole across the road. It would be foolish to drive anywhere in those conditions. She went to the front door and stood outside the house to confirm that it was as bad as it looked from the window. It would be foolish even to go for a walk, she thought, and wondered what the hell to do with her long-anticipated day off.

She sat at the table and opened her airmail pad to re-read a half-written letter to her mother who was nursing in Saudi Arabia on a very lucrative contract. Celia's father lived in Wicklow with a younger woman and she rarely saw either parent. Her mother had invited Celia to meet her in Malta for Christmas, and she was trying to compose a pleasant refusal. She had no desire at all to leave Bally C just as she was settling in. Christmas in Bally C sounded fun. The crowd in Lily's were planning to have a cabaret evening, a popular annual event. The prospect of spending Christmas alone did not worry Celia. She had often faced the same prospect when teaching abroad, and something always seemed to turn up.

She abandoned the letter. Not in the mood. A few pints might improve things. Against the economy rules, but why the hell not? She was at last making some money to supplement her savings, and she believed she wrote a more amusing letter after a few pints.

It was one o'clock when she headed down the road to Lily's. There was a seat on the front bench between Ian and Ben. Each person sitting up there greeted her in turn:

'Celia,' and she replied, 'Lily, Ian, Ben, Charlie, Daniel, Clarissa, Boris.'

'Filthy weather.'

'You could choke in it.'

'No sign of it lifting.'

'Bantry's off then.'

'Unless you're feeling suicidal.'

'Shit.'

* * *

'Let's play poker.'
Silence.

'Okay, let's *not* play poker.'
'Great idea.'
Silence.

'It's the last day of the Monty Python too.'
'It would be, wouldn't it?'
'Reminds me of their version of *All Things Bright and Beautiful.*'
'For Christ's sake Ian, not again.'
'I haven't heard it.'
'It's painful. He can't remember the words.'
'It goes something like: All things sick and cancerous
All evil great and small
All things green and gangrenous
The Lord God made them all . . .

and it goes on like that . . . each little snake that poisons, each little wasp that stings . . . then later on it has this great line: Who made the sharks? *HE* did!'
'Great! It's exactly that sort of day.'
'Yeah . . . Who made the sharks?'
'*HE* did!'

Eventually Ben got a poker game going and they played in the back room until six o'clock when Daniel and Charlie had to leave. Fanny and Ownie were at home cooking a meal for them.

Nobody else left, though each felt that they should: Celia to finish her letter, Clarissa to work, Ben to avoid getting drunk and Ian to milk his goats. Instead they sat up at the front bench again and watched the second wave of Saturday trade arriving. Each newcomer greeted Lily with a report on the state of the mist. From these they gathered that it was very localised, but still as thick as ever in patches. Nobody felt like attempting the drive to Bantry along fifteen miles of mountainy roads.

Instead they stayed in Lily's until closing time.

Celia and Ian went up their road together in the milky light of the one street lamp, walking with exaggerated caution and giggling. They stopped at her front door and Ian waited as Celia turned the key in the latch and pushed the door open with a bang of her shoulder.

She knew the next move was up to her. Invite him in for a cup of tea. Then he'd stay the night in warm comforting physical closeness. Companionable and uncomplicated relief. She hesitated. Maybe Ian didn't fancy her. Better to wait for him to make the first move.

' 'Night Ian.'

He hovered, then backed away into the misty shadows.

'Sleep tight luv.'

''Night.'

She slammed the door behind her and flicked on the light bulb that hung in the centre of her front room. Her unfinished letter lay on the table. The curtains were undrawn. The stove had gone out and the mist seemed to have seeped indoors. The place looked shabby and un-cared for. Its silence rang in Celia's ears.

As she glanced through the window she saw a figure in an oversized army parka silhouetted against the streetlamp. It was Clarissa. She peered into the window, saw Celia standing alone at the table, and ran on up the road towards *Château Despair*. Celia understood then. It was not that Ian didn't fancy her: he was spoken for. But she'd never have guessed that he was involved with Clarissa. She wondered if Ben knew.

The depression and lack of purpose which had made her

flee to Lily's and had kept her there so long, returned at double strength. Too listless to eat, she boiled a kettle for her hot water bottle and dragged herself upstairs to bed, longing for the solace that only the unconsciousness of sleep could bring.

Next day Celia did not go to Lily's for a lunchtime drink. She worked hard at her baking instead and made herself a meal from the left-over scraps. By three-thirty she had finished the final batch of pasties and decided to go off on a kindling walk in the hour or so that remained before dusk.

She passed Lily coming into Bally C as she left. They greeted each other without stopping.

'Hallo, Celia.'

'Lily. How're you keeping?'

'I'm grand. We missed you earlier.'

'I was baking.'

'It's grand weather for a walk.'

'It is.'

The mist had been dispersed by a fresh southerly wind which blew in straight off the Atlantic, carrying small clouds across the clear blue sky with its gusts. The south wind always brought good weather to Bally C, being neither wet like the prevailing southwest wind nor cold like the northeast.

Celia decided to follow the road as far as Ardbeigh, an abandoned tin-mining settlement to the east of Bally C. There were several cliff paths at Ardbeigh giving access to a south-facing strand which looked out over the islands of Roaring Water Bay. It was a popular place in the summer with those who knew how to find it, but at this time of year it should be deserted, and might have good driftwood pickings.

She waved at Ian as she passed *Château Despair*. He was reclining in the caravan's picture-window with a bottle of beer and a Sunday tabloid.

Autumn came late to Bally C, just as summer came earlier than to the rest of Ireland. Trees were only now shedding their leaves in quantity, their rust colours toning in with the russet clumps of dry bracken in the roadside banks. As the leaves started to fall, berries became easier to spot. Celia suspected that she was looking at bushes laden with great quantities of sloes and she wished that she knew for certain. She would ask Emily later that week when she went up to pull her leeks.

Ardbeigh was a bleak spot at first sight. The mine's two tall brick chimneys were still standing, and a few hundred yards from their base was a row of ruined north-facing cottages. The ground was mostly gravel and did not support much plant life beyond the tougher sea grasses. The road running past Ardbeigh to a couple of farms was tarmacked but badly pitted. The sea was not visible from the road, and many strangers passed by the place without ever discovering the chain of coves that lay below the ruins.

Celia surveyed the coves from above before choosing a path that emerged down on the shore nearest the best scattering of driftwood. It was low tide, and a strand of firm sand was exposed below the rocky shingle, temporarily linking the three coves.

She soon had her two bags filled with kindling, but the supply of bleached misshapen logs was so plentiful that she decided to make a pile of them at the top of the cliff and collect them later in her car. She had not discussed fuel with Jimmy, but assumed that once his logs were finished (which they were about to be) it would be up to her to replace them.

Her almost daily walks over hilly countryside had left Celia fitter than she had been for years. Her weight had not gone down much, according to the scales in the pharmacy at Skibbereen, but she felt that she carried it better.

The effort of scrambling up and down the cliffside and the satisfaction at the pile of wood accumulating on top combined with the mild southerly wind and a gentle sifting sound coming from the bay to lull Celia into a mildly euphoric state. So concentrated was she on her mechanical task that at first she did not notice people gathering near the ruined cottages. It was only when two unfamiliar cars drew up that she stopped to look in that direction.

Four men got out of each car, and two dogs. A motorcycle drew up and two men dismounted. They hailed a straggling group who emerged from the lee of the cottages. And every single man was carrying a gun.

Rifles, Celia thought.

They had not seen her, she was sure of that. She dropped her logs and scrambled back down the cliff. There was something very sinister about it all. So many armed men gathering together so far away from anywhere. She could not imagine what was going on. But, whatever it was, she was sure that her presence would not be welcomed. She stayed perfectly still leaning against and rock and breathing heavily.

She was bewildered. Surely nothing subversive could be happening so close to Bally C? Nothing political . . .

In the distance she heard horses' hooves. On the strand. Coming in her direction.

At a gallop.

She closed her eyes.

Her innocent little jaunt was acquiring the surreal illogic of a bad dream.

The rider was crouched up over the horse's neck and had his eyes straight ahead. Celia opened hers in time to see him pass the rocks that separated her from the next cove and the end of the strand. Then a shout of 'Whhoooooaaa!' was carried back to her. The gallop slowed to a trot, and Jimmy, still leaning forward out of the saddle, reappeared around the headland.

She took a step towards him and waved. He turned his mount in Celia's direction and trotted her up the strand.

'Celia! Fine day!'

'It is.' Her knees were weak and she was trembling.

'What brings you out here?'

She forced a nonchalant reply, hoping to delay Jimmy long enough to broach the subject of the armed men without seeming hysterical.

'Oh, I was fetching kindling, and I found a few logs. I thought I'd come back for them later . . .'

'You'd best stick to the road on your way home. The gun club's meeting above at the mines for some kind of organised shoot.'

'Oh, is that what it is?' She felt stupid and greatly relieved. Some of the fields she passed on her walks were labelled with signs saying "Lands Preserved – Bally C Gun Club", but this was the first time she'd come across any of its members in action.

Jimmy laughed, but not at her fright as Celia thought.

'What are you doing out here picking up logs? I've a rake of them up at Bawnavota, I'll bring a load down to you tomorrow in the trailer.'

'Oh. Thanks.' She walked up to the mare, a good-looking chestnut, and reached out to stroke her nose. The mare tossed her head and took three prancing steps to the side. Celia dodged back out of her way.

'Gerrawayoutathat,' said Jimmy in an affectionate voice. 'She's still excited from the gallop and she's not used to being petted.' He reached forward and stroked her neck. 'Yer savage.'

'What's her name?'

'Southerly Strand. I named her for this place.'

'It's a lovely name. And she's a real beauty.'

'Oh aye. She'd have the country robbed by her looks, as they used to say long ago. She's yet to win a race, the lazy bag'a'bones.' He patted her again and said, 'Con tells me you're a bit of a horsewoman yourself.'

'I haven't ridden for ages, but I'd love to.'

'How about tomorrow morning?'

'Tomorrow?'

'I've four horses in work at the moment, three of my own and Con's mare. You'd be doing me a favour.'

'That's wonderful but . . .'

'Have you a crash helmet?'

'No . . .'

'We'll fix you up.' He turned the mare and started to walk away. 'She'll be getting cold standing about . . . I'll see you up at Con's place at half-eight.'

'Half-eight?' A dozen questions were forming in her mind.

'Some of us around here get out of bed before noon you know.' He smiled at her then shouted over his shoulder, 'We'll be through by half-ten and you've the rest of the day to go baking.'

Celia had once owned a pair of riding breeches, but could not remember when or where she had jettisoned them. Perhaps they were in the attic of her father's house along with her hard hat, her riding crop and a trunkful of other discards. If this riding business worked out she'd write and ask him to search.

She'd noticed that Jimmy and Con both rode in their working gumboots, so she decided to do the same. That, and her second best jeans, which she was pleased to find were now baggy on the hips and at least an inch too big in the waist, her black crew-neck sweater which she wore all the time and, stroke of brilliance, her hacking jacket. The latter was a fashion item, some years out-moded, tailored from viscose-simulated tweed, but at least, Celia thought, it *looked* right.

She laid her clothes out on her bedside chair before going to bed.

Even though she was looking forward to the morning, she did not sleep well. She planned to get up at seven thirty, two hours earlier than usual. Her alarm clock was unreliable: she had forgotten to replace it before leaving London and this was the first time she'd needed to rise early since arriving in Bally C. To oversleep would be humiliating, especially after Jimmy's condescending remark on the strand.

On Southerly Strand.

Celia wondered which mount she would get, and tried to remember everything she knew about riding. Mount and dismount from the left side (as seen from the top). Face the tail to mount. Grip with the knees, heels down, toes in, elbows in, hands down, reins through little finger, gather up reins and kick on to trot, rise to the trot, kick on, shorten reins, sit to the canter, pull back and down to stop . . . and the seat, she'd often been told she had a good seat . . . as Con said, a child could do it . . .

She woke at six after a series of disturbing dreams which left no memory. She opened the curtains and removed her eiderdown, hoping the chill would prevent another deep sleep. Then she dozed intermittently as the dawn light strengthened.

She got up at seven fifteen and stood for a few minutes looking out over the grey stillness of the mountains from her staircase window. It was a new picture for her, and a calming one.

Celia parked in the road beside the blackthorn bush and walked on up Con's boreen. She had allowed ten minutes for this, considering it preferable to the risk of getting stuck again.

It was now almost full light. The sky was slightly overcast, and threatening rain. Celia stayed on the grass verge of the boreen, and noticed more berries, probably sloes, in its tall banks. She'd not had time to ask Emily about them yet.

The lane seemed far longer than she'd remembered and she was starting to worry that she'd misjudged the time when she caught sight of Jimmy's Land Rover at the foot of the hill.

He was crossing the yard carrying two empty buckets and greeted her with a cheerful smile.

'Hallo there! My, what a smart turn-out.'

He was looking at her jacket.

'You wouldn't want to be ruining a nice jacket like that riding out. You should save it for the hunter trials.'

'Oh, it's an old thing. I don't mind what happens to it.'

'I'm afraid we're not very smart around here. We ride out in our work clothes.'

'That's fine.'

Jimmy seemed amused, and Celia was not sure how to take his teasing.

'They're both fed and tacked up,' he said. 'We'll go over and see if Con's ready for us.'

They walked the few yards up to Con's place as he was leading Dún Donncha out of the yard. He nodded to Celia and Jimmy and stopped in front of his house. Jimmy went over and gave him a leg-up. Once he was in the saddle Con turned to Celia: 'Grand morning for a spin if the rain holds off.'

'It is.'

Con turned to the right, and Jimmy started walking in the opposite direction, back to the stables. Celia followed Jimmy.

'Where's he going?'

'He'll just walk him round the field till we're ready. He's a holy terror, that Con. He shouldn't be up on a horse at all, let alone a stone-mad savage like Dún Donncha.'

'Why ever not?'

Jimmy sounded frustrated, as if Celia had asked the most stupid question he'd ever heard. 'Jesus, he's a leg held together by nuts and bolts for five years now. Didn't you notice the limp?'

'Yes, a slight one. I thought it was arthritis.'

'Smashed to bits in a car crash, that's why he's no car. He won't drive cars any more. It was head on, the two girls in the other car died. Nurses from the Regional. And it left Barney Mack with a buzzing in the ears and blinding headaches.'

'How awful.'

'He's a stupid eejit but you can't keep him away from the horses. Yerra, I'd probably be the same way myself in his state.' Jimmy's face softened and his eyes took on a gentle look which Celia had noticed once before – on the strand, when he had patted his mare.

They were back at the loose boxes, Jimmy paused.

'So you've done a bit of riding before?'

'I had lots of lessons when I was a kid. I haven't ridden regularly since I was about fourteen, but I've been out a few times.' Then she added quickly, 'But I've never ridden horses as nice as yours, never anything thoroughbred.'

Jimmy laughed, 'Oh, I know. Tired old riding-school hacks that'd find their way round the park with a sack of potatoes on their back. I tried them a few times when I lived in London.'

This was news. Celia had never suspected that Jimmy had lived in London, but then she'd never asked.

'I'm putting you up on Southerly Strand. She had a good work-out yesterday, so she shouldn't be too fresh. But keep her on a tight rein, keep a good hold on her mouth.'

'Okay.' Celia was nervous, and she looked it.

'She's quiet as a lamb on the roads, you'll have no need to worry about traffic. Can you rise to the trot?'

'Oh aye.'

'Well, we won't do anything more than a quiet trot up the hill with them this morning. You shouldn't find it too much of a strain.'

He led Southerly Strand out of her box and indicated that Celia should put her knee in his hands for a leg-up. Before

Celia could reflect on how tall and strong the animal looked, she was in the saddle.

'First lesson,' said Jimmy, 'Get a hold of the reins before I hoist you so that you'll be in control from the minute you're in the saddle.'

Celia nodded.

'Jeez, I forgot the hats. Hang on there a minute.'

Celia grasped the reins with both hands, gripped with her knees, and willed Southerly Strand to stay still. The stirrup leathers seemed too short, otherwise she liked the feel of being in the saddle.

Jimmy came back carrying two whitish crash helmets. He handed the newest-looking one to Celia.

'Try that. I'll hold her while you put it on.'

'That's fine thanks.'

'It's back to front.'

'Oh God.' Celia stopped trying to fasten the chip strap and turned the hat the other way round. 'That's better.'

'Don't worry, I won't tell a soul.' Jimmy laughed again.

'I always had a hard hat,' said Celia.

'Those shagging things are useless, they should be banned.' He was looking at her critically. She wondered what else she'd done wrong.

'I suppose the leathers are too short?'

'Yes, they are a bit.'

'Pull your leg back. There. Better?'

'Fine.' He went around to the other side and adjusted the second leather.

'Same length?'

'I think so. Hang on . . . yes.'

'Let me tighten the girth and we're off. I'll warn you now, I'm no riding master. Just grip with your knees and keep a good hold of the reins. That's about all the learning you'll get from me.'

Jimmy led a chestnut gelding into the yard and vaulted

into the saddle. He walked him out into the lane, and Southerly Strand followed. Con and Dún Donncha were waiting beside the Land Rover.

'What kept ya?' he called out. Jimmy ignored him.

Dún Donncha jogged past Jimmy and Celia and walked up the boreen ahead of them followed by four setters and the aged springer spaniel. Celia soon dropped behind Jimmy. He turned a couple of times to look at her and then shouted 'Okay there?'

'Fine.'

And she was.

She had relaxed almost immediately into the rhythm of the mare, forgetting her attack of nerves, and felt comfortable and easy in the saddle. The mare seemed quiet enough and kept her ears pricked forward, which Celia judged to be a sign of good temper.

Being up on the mare's back gave Celia a different view of the countryside. She felt a new freedom and a certain superiority as she surveyed the rough fields beyond the dykes of the boreen.

They turned to the left at the road, passing her car. She noticed a seagull's dropping on its roof. There was some shouted exchange between Jimmy and Con which she was too far behind to hear. She dug her heels into the mare's flanks and clicked with her tongue to urge her forward. The mare jogged on, and Celia, who had forgotten to grip with her knees, flopped about in the saddle.

'Whoa!' She pulled her up behind Jimmy.

'We're turning left here then we'll trot on up the hill,' he said.

'Fine.'

Con turned first, then Jimmy, then Celia. Southerly Strand was reluctant to trot, so Celia kicked her harder, gathering the reins up through her fingers. She was away, trotting nicely and rising to it.

Southerly Strand trotted faster, closing the gap between

Celia and Jimmy, and trotted on past Jimmy, catching up with Dún Donncha. Celia smiled apologetically at Jimmy as she passed, and tried to slow the mare by pulling back on the reins. She could already feel herself tiring from the unaccustomed exertion.

Then, as the Strand's head came up to Dún Donncha's hindquarters, she broke into a canter. Celia pulled back on the reins and sat down in the saddle, confident that she could slow her. Southerly Strand ignored the feeble little tugs on her mouth and streaked past Dún Donncha.

'Whoa! Whoa!' Celia shouted and tugged.

Southerly Strand swerved towards the grass verge, almost leaving Celia in a heap on the tarmac. But she gripped and stayed on and she shouted louder, not caring that her voice now had a tone of panic instead of one of firm command?

'Whoa! Whoa! STOP! ST-O-O-P! WHOOOOAAA!'

The reins slipped through her fingers as the mare took the bit, and Celia clung to the low pommel of the saddle, still sitting well back. Again her balance went, and she was flung forward onto the mare's neck. She managed to grab the reins again, one in each fist, and held on to them halfway down the mane.

The mare must tire soon, and Celia was determined to stick on her back at any cost. She could see the crest of the hill about a hundred yards ahead, and she remembered vaguely that horses did not like galloping downhill – or was it people who did not like horses to gallop downhill . . .

She clung, and tried not to think about the hardness of the tarmac flashing past below her eyes, just slightly to her right, nor of the possibility of holes in the grass verge. All her concentration was spent on staying on, her muscles inflamed by a tiny picture of a white-crash-helmeted person in a smart tweed jacket lying senseless in the middle of the road. It was not going to be her.

At the top of the hill Celia made one more big effort to

pull back on the reins, with no result. But now she had her balance again, her seat was out of the saddle, her hands clinging to Southerly Strand's mane, a rein in each hand, and, whatever else, she was going to stay on.

Far below, at the bottom of the hill, she could see a pink farmhouse and whitewashed outbuildings. The road widened at the farm, and she would try, down there, to turn the mare, only stay on that far, and surely . . .

Her sweating hands slipped on the mane. She lost the reins again and almost fell off, but her knees still kept a grip somehow, and she gave a great shout of fury and fear –

'WHOOOOOOAAA!'

– and then, just as her little remaining strength was giving out the mare slowed to a gentle trot.

She yanked on the right rein and Southerly Strand slowed to a walk just as they approached the farmyard. The Strand came to a halt, then she ambled across the road to the opposite grass verge and started to munch grass.

Celia sank her head down on to the mane, dropped the reins, stayed there for a long moment, then collapsed back into the saddle exhausted.

Exhausted, but still in the saddle.

She turned Southerly Strand back in the direction they had come, but the mare did not want to walk on. She continued to graze. Celia was too exhausted to pull the mare's head up again from the grass and would not risk kicking her on. Instead they stood on the verge and waited.

There was no sign of Jimmy and Con. Celia could not even hear hoofbeats. She was almost sure she had not passed a turning off. In any case wouldn't they be worried about her, or at least about the mare? Would Jimmy be furious because she'd galloped on the road? Celia knew it could damage a horse's legs. In the riding schools that she had known the gallop was a forbidden pace altogether.

She started to worry that this might be her last ride with

Jimmy. Instead of relief at such a short-lived equestrian career, she found the idea bitterly disappointing. She did not want to be rejected so soon. Even in her current state of shock and exhaustion she wanted another chance. Because she knew that she could, and given the chance, would, do better. Much better.

The setters were first in view, running along the grass verge, then she saw Con and Jimmy coming over the crest of the hill before she heard their hoofbeats. They walked towards her talking between themselves. She pulled the Strand's head up from the grass and waited for the worst.

Southerly Strand started to fidget and Celia let her walk on up the hill towards the other two horses.

'Still aboard? Good girl,' shouted Jimmy.

(Good girl! How dare he?) 'I'm terribly sorry, she ran away with me . . .

'Oh aye, it happens.' Jimmy did not seem in the least upset nor excited. 'She's used to racing Dún Donncha, and she musta thought she was out for another run like she had yesterday. You'd have to be a strong man to hold her when she's a mind to go.'

(Strong man! Fat bloody chance I've got of being a strong man! And he might have warned me, the bastard.)

Con walked up beside her on Dún Donncha and smiled: 'She give 'oo a good spin, the hoor, and 'oo stuckonner. Yerra fine gerral. I tell 'oo.'

That was more like it. Celia glowed with satisfaction. Con was a gentleman and Jimmy was a cold, condescending bastard.

About half a mile beyond the farm where Celia and Southerly Strand had halted, the road they were following met a busier road at a T junction. Two overladen beet trucks passed them at speed, and Celia realised just how lucky she had been that Southerly Strand had stopped where she did. She was also surprised at how calmly the horses let the trucks roar past them. When travelling in single file at a walk Jimmy's description of the Strand as 'quiet as a lamb' was accurate.

Even though she had regained some confidence on the walk home, Celia was glad when they finally arrived at the yard. She staggered on dismounting, her knees numb. Jimmy led his mount into a box and then took Southerly Strand from Celia.

'Are you on for another spin?'

'Another?'

'I've a new bay half-broken and it'd be a help if you were up on Bally C Lady. It might teach the bay some manners. We'll give them about twenty minutes work in the field.'

'Okay.'

She'd been wanting another chance, an opportunity to show some competence, and here it was. Her stiffness and exhaustion disappeared as she summoned all the energy she could find to face the challenge. Perhaps there was some logic in Jimmy's coldness and casualness. His lack of concern for her well-being inspired her to an uncharacteristic bravado.

'Take this lot over to Con's yard and he'll tack her up for you.'

He stuck the saddle on Celia's outstretched arm and hung the bridle and martingale over her other shoulder. The underside of the saddle was still damp with the Strand's sweat. Celia liked the strong smell of horse.

Bally C Lady was smaller than Southerly Strand and did not pull as hard. Celia preferred the feel of the Lady and was sure that she could handle this mare better.

Con stood outside his barn and watched as Celia and Jimmy walked the horses around the edge of the big field beyond his house.

Con's field, where Jimmy did most of his schooling, was oblong with a slight uphill slope on the shorter sides. There was a jump in the middle of the top straight, but the bay was not yet ready to tackle that obstacle so Jimmy steered to the inside of the field to pass it.

After circling the field twice at a walk and once at a trot Jimmy pulled the bay up in the bottom right-hand corner, and waited for Celia to catch up with him.

'A'right there?'

'Fine. She's a sweetie.'

'I'd like to give them a slow canter up the hill, across on the diagonal. You keep behind me and I'll set the pace. Keep a good hold of her, but she won't pull the arms off you like the Strand. Ready?'

Celia gathered up the reins and kicked the Lady on. She trotted, then went into a slow easy canter. For a few moments Celia felt perfectly at one with the mare, in control and enjoying the motion.

Then something went wrong with the bay. She saw Jimmy rise out of the saddle and fall on to the bay's neck at an awkward angle as the bay broke into a gallop and headed off up the field.

And Bally C Lady was going to follow. Celia knew that slightly before it happened, but as the mare gathered speed something else went wrong and this time Celia gave up. She knew she was going to fall off: there was no point in struggling. Instead she relaxed and watched as if hypnotised while the tufty grass beneath the mare came closer and closer to her face. There was a thump as the field came up to hit her, she lost all orientation for a moment, and then she knew that she was off. And she was clear, and there was no pain. She rolled over once, then, when the field had stopped moving, she stood up slowly, slightly dazed, and saw Con limping towards her with a look of great concern on his face.

'I'm okay,' she shouted. 'Get the mare.'

Then she looked towards the top of the field and saw Jimmy's bay standing at the top left corner, riderless. Bally C Lady was beside her.

She and Con ran up the slope and arrived at the corner

panting as Jimmy scrambled out of a hedge. Blood was trickling down his face.

'You a'right?' he asked Celia.

'Fine. I fell clear.' She was, however, still trembling and dazed.

'She bucked 'oo off,' said Con.

'Did she?'

'The bay give a buck and took off and the hoor has to go doing the same thing. The Lady'd never have thrown 'oo on her own, I tell 'oo.'

Celia was entranced. She had not fallen off, she had been *thrown*. It made all the difference: it was not feebleness nor incompetence on her part, but something that could have happened any day to a far more experienced rider.

'The new bay is a right hoor,' said Jimmy in a grim voice. 'Did you see what she did to me?'

Con was laughing now, convulsively: 'I see 'oo, I see 'oo,' was all that he could manage to say.

Jimmy explained to Celia, 'I stayed on a'right when she bucked but I lost a rein and the hoor goes off at a gallop and stands on the brakes at the very edge of the field so I go straight over her head and into the fucking dyke. Third fucking time in a week I've been in it.'

Celia tried not to laugh at his indignation, but Con's fit of mirth was irresistible. Even Jimmy had to smile as he mopped at his face with a filthy handkerchief, 'Three fucking times in one week.'

'I see 'oo.' Con was still at it.

'Let's have a look at your cut,' said Celia.

'Yerra it's just a scratch offa the brambles. I musta hit them at thirty-five miles an hour.'

Con was holding the two mares.

'I'm going to make that horse take the hill at a canter if it kills me.' Jimmy was walking towards the bay. He turned and looked at Celia. She knew this was it. If she refused to get up on the Lady again she might as well forget about riding for Jimmy or for anyone else.

'I'm on,' she said, joining him beside the mares.

'Good girl.' He slapped her back and she staggered. 'You've more spirit than most.'

He gave her a leg-up and they walked across the top of the field and back down to the corner and tried again. This time all was perfect, and Celia, though nervous and exhausted, arrived at the top corner of the field glowing with something beyond the usual exhilaration of a good canter.

She walked the mare back to Con's yard triumphant.

In winter Clarissa often took long solitary walks. Her tall figure wrapped in a large US army parka that came down to her knees was a familiar sight around Roaring Water Bay. A three-hour circuit was not unusual for her. In her pockets she carried a bar of chocolate which she always ate *en route*, and a notebook which she seldom used. If the weather was fine she'd often stop and sit on top of a metal five-bar gate looking out to sea past the islands. If it was wet, as it so often was, she pulled her hood over her head and drew her hands up into the shelter of her long sleeves and walked faster.

Her walks and the long mornings spent lying in bed dozing were as much a part of her work schedule as the daily minimum of two hours at the table in her workroom. At the table she wrote, but the only reason that she knew what to write was, as she understood it, because the apparent mindlessness of both dozing and walking allowed her thoughts to settle in a pattern that made them accessible to words. It was her way of digesting her experiences and sifting the useful from the trivial. And the harder she 'worked' (i.e. dozing and walking) the less trivia there seemed to be in her life.

This made perfect sense to Clarissa, but she was having trouble explaining it to Jimmy. He was just in from a good day's hunting and warming himself up with a hot whiskey. Clarissa was engaged in a similar operation following a three-hour trek along the coast road. They were Lily's only customers, hence their unprecedented *tête à tête*.

'There's no sense in it at all. Mind you, there's no harm in it either, but I can't see the sense. If it's exercise you want you could go shooting with Ben and you'd have something to show for it.'

'But it's not just the exercise. It helps me to write, it's work. Shooting's a distraction, I don't need any distractions. And anyway I don't like killing things.'

'You should try riding out. Now that's the best exercise of all . . .'

'I hate horses. They terrify me.'

'But you don't like shooting things?'

'Just because I don't like animals it doesn't mean I have to go around killing them.'

'But you eat what Ben kills?'

'That's different. By the time it's been plucked and drawn and roasted it's *food*. Why do you think we have a different word for cattle and beef?'

'But a pheasant's a pheasant whether it's on my land or on my table.'

Clarissa looked at him with such contempt that Jimmy decided it was time to stop his teasing. He had not intended to provoke her. He was merely curious.

Clarissa and Ben had long been a puzzle to Jimmy, but not one that he had shown much interest in until recently. Con had come up with a well-nigh incredible story about Clarissa. Con was not given to fantasies, especially not erotic fantasies, nor to boasting, but Jimmy found his tale hard to believe. Jimmy of course knew many women who enjoyed casual sex, but Clarissa did not strike him as the sort of person who would do so with Con. With Jimmy himself, yes, but why did she make such an odd choice as Con? West Cork's bachelor farmers are not known for their amorous sublety. Jimmy guessed that Clarissa was an adventurer, wild enough to try anything once. If Con had, as he claimed, been there, then it was a challenge to Jimmy to get there too.

Jimmy had found that he enjoyed Ben's company. The loud-mouthed Yank (as he thought of him) improved on acquaintance. Neither Jimmy nor Ben belonged to the Bally C Gun Club and much of their shooting was, technically, poaching. Ben, who had more time than Jimmy to pursue that sport, was generous with good tips on the current location of birds, and Jimmy had suggested that the two of them shoot together with his dogs one evening soon. A certain old-fashioned sense of propriety made Jimmy want to get the Clarissa business out of the way before consolidating his friendship with Ben.

Jimmy called for a third hot whiskey which he did not really want in order to prolong his conversation with Clarissa. A change of topic was obviously in order.

'There's a southerly on its way. Gale force 9, imminent, they said on the radio.'

'Bloody gales.'

'I'd have thought you found them inspiring.'

(O God. Why do they all think I go around getting 'inspired'? Can't even talk about the weather without *that* . . .)

'I find gales cold and wet and noisy. Just like anyone else.'

'Did you ever hear the out-haul in a southerly?'

(The out-haul. That dreadful roaring and sucking sound as the tide drags around the islands in the bay . . .)

'Did I ever hear the out-haul? What the hell do you think keeps me awake all bloody night in a gale even through the double-glazing?'

'Ah, that's no way to hear the out-haul. You have to be down on the strand with the moonlight on. I tell you, even I'd go writing poems below on a night like this.'

Clarissa caught a new tone in Jimmy's voice. Suggestive, certainly, but also very romantic.

'Below where?'

'On Southerly Strand.'

'Where's that?'

'You'd know it by sight, if not by name. I'll take you there. There's a full moon tonight. But I don't want you to go telling anyone else about it.'

(Us, or Southerly Strand? Intriguing . . .)

'Oh aye?'

'Meet me up at the Hilton at ten o'clock. Just yourself.'

'I'll think about it.'

Working the horses transformed Celia's life. It seemed she had never been so busy before, nor so pleasantly tired at the end of the day. She still had the pasties to bake, and two big pâtés a week to cook for the delicatessen. She went less often to Lily's, and when she did she usually ended up talking horses with Con and Jimmy. She looked forward to going up to Emily's place, Clogheen, in the late afternoon to pull her leeks, and sometimes stayed to tea with Emily and the children, lingering on to chat to them over a pot of tea or a bottle of home-made wine after reading a bed-time story to Edward.

Her enquiries about the sloe berries reminded Emily of her one remaining bottle of sloe poitín, so Celia stayed on that evening to sample it. Both women were sitting with their feet in the warming oven of Emily's range sipping the powerful brew from egg cups on which the words 'Souvenir of Ballycashlinacosta' had been scrawled in a downward spiral. The General had drawn up plans to lay down another batch with Celia supplying the berries and half the price of the hooch.

She had discovered that outside Lily's and away from Clarissa the General could be very good company. Celia liked Emily's toughness and her independence, and admired her many abilities. She also liked observing her no-nonsense handling of the children, who were often engaged in their outdoor chores while Celia was pulling leeks. Celia did not usually enjoy children, but she had become very fond of Aoife and Edward. They were both remarkably self-assured, and talked to adults on adult's terms, but they had quite distinct characters. Edward showed a sweetness and vulnerability which were lacking in his elder sister. Aoife was remarkably beautiful and extremely intelligent and she knew it.

Emily refilled their egg cups with sloe poitín. 'This is the time of day I like best', she said. 'The kids are in bed, the chores are all done, and the stove's throwing out a decent bit of heat.'

'Oh aye,' said Celia, who'd risen at seven fifteen that morning to ride out, 'there's nothing like a well-earned rest.'

'I think that's why I like November so much, the long dark evenings. In summer I can stay out there working till ten or eleven, I just keep going as long as there's light and then drop.'

'I don't know how you stick it.'

'Because I like it, I suppose. But I've often thought of selling up. Sometimes I think it's not really fair on the kids living here . . . it's great for them in some ways, but in other ways . . . I mean, Aoife wants to take ballet classes . . .'

'Ballet classes? Why doesn't she learn to ride instead?'

'Sod's law. She wants ballet classes. She got a medal for Irish dancing last term down at the school and now she thinks she's destined for stardom. I've been teaching her belly dancing, but that's not good enough.'

Emily caught Celia's astonished glance and went on. 'I learnt to belly dance while I was at university, it's not just for fat women in the harem, you know. It's wonderful relaxation. Anyway, Aoife insists on ballet classes. The nearest ballet class is in Bantry, that's a thirty-mile round trip, and I'm damned if I'm doing that every Saturday just so that she can go leaping around in a tutu. And it's going to get worse the older they get.'

'I suppose boarding school's out of the question.'

'That's what their father wants, English boarding schools of course, and there's a slight chance that he might persuade my mother-in-law to pay for most of it . . . you know what it would cost per term for the two of them? More than I make in a year I reckon. Anyway, I think it's a cop-out. They have a perfectly good home here with me. That's what I work for.'

'Well, they seem to like it. And I think it's ideal for children.'

'That's the idea. Look, if I sold this place, I mean suppose anyone would be nuts enough to buy it, I'd probably just about manage to buy a two-bedroom flat in London. Can you imagine? And what sort of job could I get? As far as employers are concerned I'm just another arts graduate with no work experience. *This* doesn't count for anything.' She paused to look around her and gestured with a wave of her arm at the room.

Apart from a scullery area and a pantry, the ground floor of the farmhouse consisted of one large room. A heavy curtain was drawn across the middle to keep out draughts from the staircase and the sitting-room area so Emily's gesture only included the kitchen. It was dominated by a large wooden table, one third of which was kept clear for eating. The rest of it was cluttered with books, letters, bills, jam jars and sauce bottles, bits of knitting, paper bags and all kinds of odds and ends; even, Celia noticed, a couple of sparking plugs. But the rest of the kitchen was a model of organisation with Emily's equipment neatly stacked in open shelves along the walls: cheese-making bowls and presses, wine-making equipment, cooking pots, baking dishes and loaf tins and old fashioned delft which she picked up cheap or free when she could. Some of her veterinary drugs and syringes were up on the highest shelves, bunches of dried herbs hung from the ceiling and there were enough jars of pickles and chutneys and jams to stock a small grocer. Beside the range were a tall stack of old newspapers and a rush basket full of kindling, while several gallon jars of wine were fermenting away above the range. Under the superficial chaos, the place was more like a multi-purpose factory than a kitchen.

'A two-bedroomed flat! Can you imagine?' Emily looked around again and shook her head. 'When I weigh *that* against *this*, with all and the lack of fucking ballet classes, then I'm sure I'm not being selfish. I mean, they have friends, and the school is excellent apart from the damn religion, they have a nice home, the animals, good food, fresh air, open space . . . they're doing the flower garden for me next year.' She picked up a tattered seed catalogue from the table and handed it to Celia. 'Heavy on nasturtiums and sunflowers I believe. Edward loves toasted sunflower seeds and Aoife's mad about pickled nasturtium pods. Kids are always extremely self-interested when they decide to co-operate. Have another drop of hooch – I've got Ben and Clarissa coming up for supper tomorrow and I doubt the bottle will survive that.'

Celia held out her glass. It was going to her head, but she was enjoying it.

'I had the most extraordinary conversation with Clarissa the other day,' said Celia.

'Oh aye.' Emily picked up a half-finished sock, part of her winter quota for Boris.

'Does she screw around a lot?'

'Oh aye. Compulsively.' Emily sounded disgusted.

'That would explain it. She accosted me outside the Post Office and told me that she'd found the cure for promiscuity.'

'Oh aye.'

'If you fancy someone you have to ask yourself whether it's love, lust or romance, and if it's not at least two of them, forget it.'

'Hah. That's probably a line from one of her poems. She was trying it out on you. A cure for promiscuity's the last thing she wants at the moment. She's having a whale of a time.'

'Do you like Clarissa?'

'Oh, I don't think "like" is the word. I just accept her as being totally impossible. Maybe even a bit of a looney, but a harmless one, and she can be quite funny. Some of her verse is very good actually. This screwing-around business is a new thing with her, it's only since the summer. She and Ben had a bit of a fling with another couple on Ben's yacht and now they're supposed to be experimenting with an "open relationship" – very old hat, if you ask me . . . do *you* like her?'

'As you said, not exactly "like," but she's fun.'

'You put up with her because she amuses you?'

'More or less.'

Emily stopped knitting. 'I sometimes wonder whether anyone around here honestly *likes* anyone else. Maybe we all just put up with each other because that's all there is and if we didn't we'd be bored out of our skulls within a week.'

'Oh no. I like Jimmy, now that I've got used to him.'

'I wouldn't get too fond of the half-sir if I were you. Nor of his horses. He can be utterly ruthless.'

'Ruthless? Maybe. But I like Ben.'

'Ben's okay, but he's a loner. So is Clarissa. That's why they're such a mess. Has he made a pass at you yet?'

'No.'

'Well, he will sooner or later, and if I were you I'd have nothing to do with him. You've never seen him in a depression, have you? Being gross, as he calls it.'

'No.' Celia was silent for a minute, pondering over this

new information about Ben. Rather than pursue it, she decided to change the subject: 'I like Ian.'

'Oh, Ian's all right, he's a very nice lad in fact. He's been a great help to me around Clogheen. He's just a bit short on the grey matter. Bugs you after a while.'

'The Macarthys are lovely people, aren't they?' said Celia.

'Oh aye. As long as they're not fighting.'

'It's an extraordinary set-up.'

'Oh aye.'

'What are the rest of them like? The ones I haven't met.'

'Let's see. You know Charlie and Daniel and Fanny and Ownie.'

'And Marie. I met her at the party.'

'That's right. Then there's her twin Morty. He's on the oil rigs but he'll be back for Christmas. And Susan. Jimmy's ex.'

'Ex-wife?'

Emily laughed. 'No, ex-girlfriend. The half-sir has no intention of marrying anyone, ever. That's why they split up. It was just last summer. She's an absolute stunner. She's up in Dublin at the moment trying to make it as an actress and singer. That was another of the problems with Jimmy. She's hardly ever home, and when she is she just wants to be with the rest of them, so he was virtually living at Dromderrig.'

'I wouldn't think anyone'd mind that.'

'Don't be misled by that birthday party. They fight like cats and dogs most of the time. I should know, I'm their nearest neighbour and I can hear it across three fields. How do you think Daniel and Charlie lost their front teeth?'

Celia laughed. 'You know, now that I've got used to them I've noticed that they're both very good-looking in spite of the teeth.'

'They are. But for God's sake don't go falling for either of that pair. Or Morty. He's a real hunk, but he's just as much of a bastard as the other two when he loses his temper.'

'It looks as if I've got to keep my hands off all the men in Bally C,' said Celia.

'Not at all' said Emily. 'You can always go up to Con Leary for a bit of a court.'

She had intended to tell Celia about Clarissa's adventure, but changed her mind when Celia misinterpreted her flippant remark as an accusation of lechery and launched into a long defence of Con.

Jimmy modified his training schedule in such a way that, while the horses built up fitness, so did Celia. Instead of alternate road work and schooling he now gave each horse half an hour on the roads and twenty minutes or so in the field. Celia worked Bally C Lady for the full quota every day, walking her round the roads, then trotting and cantering her round the field while Jimmy rode the newly broken bay. Jimmy let her walk Southerly Strand on the roads and walk her in the field. Then, once he'd given Ardbeigh Prince half a dozen circuits at a canter, he let Celia lead the gelding up and down the boreen to cool off while he cantered Southerly Strand. Celia, who was exhausted after only two circuits of the field at a canter, envied Jimmy's fitness and admired his stamina.

Celia was encouraged by both Jimmy and Con to shorten her stirrup leathers and ride jockey-style. They liked her nerve, and appreciated her company around the yard, where she was prepared to make herself useful to them in whatever way she could. Jimmy needed the extra help, as he was often up in Cork on business. Con was too heavy to ride out anything except Dún Donncha so the horses who were in training for the point-to-point season lost fitness. If Celia could gain the competence to ride out at least the two quietest mares alone, it would be a great benefit to all concerned.

Con and Jimmy had told Celia nothing about this plan, but she was aware that, in a very low-key way, she had been put into training. One night in Lily's Con made a long speech of encouragement full of 'I tell 'oos' and suggested that she hold the reins much shorter, with her hands over halfway down the horse's neck, and cross the reins over each other in order to create a jamming effect that would increase her control. He told her to practise rising out of the saddle and gripping with her knees to find her centre of balance while walking the roads, and to try the same thing for faster paces in the field. She followed his advice and was surprised at the difference that it made.

One morning Jimmy, in a chatty offhand way, showed her how to put the bit into the horse's mouth, and next morning he watched her while she bridled the mare herself. He had already shown her how to saddle up and how to tighten her girth while in the saddle. And on the second day that she rode out she had two buckets of rolled oats thrust in her hands with instructions to deposit them in the troughs of Bally C Lady and Dún Donncha. She had no qualms about entering the mare's box: she was so docile that she stood aside to let Celia have access to the trough. Dún Donncha was blocking her entrance with his hindquarters. She had to steel her nerves against the massive unpredictable horse. She copied Con and banged her hand on the half-door and shouted '*Gerrawayoutathat*'. He moved his hindquarters, she slipped in, heart thumping, dumped the oats in the trough and was out again in a flash.

Her face was still flushed when she got back to Jimmy with the empty buckets. He smiled at her and said, 'All done? Good girl. He doesn't kick, or I'd never have sent you.' Instead of remarking sarcastically that he might have told her that before, Celia just shrugged. She was already getting used to Jimmy's ways.

Within two weeks he announced that she was now qualified to take either of 'her' mares out alone. The next time that he disappeared to Cork on business Celia was forewarned. She spent a restless night trying to decide which mare to work first, which was more likely to give trouble, and whether she wouldn't be wiser to take up Jimmy's option – 'Leave them be till I get back if you prefer.'

The young mare, Bally C Lady, was prone to shy on the roads, but was quiet and easy to handle in the field. The Strand, who was a seven-year-old, was solid as a rock on the roads, but had developed a series of what Jimmy called 'dirty tricks' in the field. Celia was supposed to counter these with a tap of her crop. The trouble was that almost every time she gave the mare a flake (as Con called it), she lost her grip on the reins and the mare took off at a canter or a gallop in whatever direction she fancied. Unlike the new bay, the Strand always slowed gradually on reaching the dyke, and as yet Celia had never come off. But the battle with the Strand wore on her nerves and combined with Bally C Lady's temperamental behaviour on the roads to keep alive the apprehension which she thought she had conquered once and for all on her first day out.

In the end Celia cheated slightly, and only gave the Strand a token work-out in the field, carrying the crop in her boot. But at least she had done it, and the next day, she resolved, she would try harder.

One morning, as Celia sat at Con's table drinking a cup of tea after working the horses, Jimmy asked if she could spare a couple more hours that morning to give him a hand.

'Oh aye. What needs doing?'

'We're going to patch up the boreen,' said Jimmy. 'It's hard labour. Maybe some of your friends would like the exercise?'

Jimmy often commented to Celia on the laziness of many of their friends. It was a rare event to see a Macarthy about before midday. Jimmy seemed to like Ben, though he always referred to him as 'the loud-mouthed Yank', but he appeared to have no time at all for Clarissa whom he had labelled 'the Bard of Bally C', nor for Ian, 'the hippie layabout'. He was especially derisive about Ian's habit of getting up around two in the afternoon.

'I suppose we could wake Ian,' said Celia. It was ten thirty.

'Lazy bollax. What does he want to lie in bed all day for?'

'He's out of work, he's got nothing to do.' Celia found some of Jimmy's attitudes over-critical. Just because *he* had reasons for getting up at the crack of dawn, there was no need to expect everyone else to do so. She herself always stayed in bed till noon on Sundays, the horses' day of rest.

'Yerra there's always something to do,' said Con.

'Like patching up your boreen. You're a fine one to talk,' said Jimmy.

'Why would I want to go patching up my boreen? Doesn't the tractor fly up and down it like a rocket?' Con chuckled.

'What about Charlie and Daniel?' said Celia.

'They've a concert up in Cork tonight so we'll let them off this time,' said Jimmy as he stood up to leave. Celia followed him. A repaired boreen would save her the walk every morning, and she considered that well worth a few hours' hard labour.

Jimmy hitched an open trailer on to his Land Rover and Celia jumped into the passenger seat. She liked the way that Jimmy drove the Land Rover, nursing its slipping clutch and steering it slowly around the worst of the pot holes. She always enjoyed doing things with Jimmy – mucking out the horses, grooming them, preparing their feeds, repairing tack, even sitting in silence at Con's table drinking cups of tea while Jimmy and Con discussed the racing pages of the *Cork Examiner*.

Jimmy did things in a slow, relaxed way, always

concentrating on the job in hand with one part of his mind, while keeping up a constant flow of conversation. Celia's picture of Jimmy had filled out. Their chats while on horseback were usually short exchanges of small talk, but even Jimmy's small talk had a novel interest for Celia. He would point out a hare sitting in the middle of a field, or a group of oyster-catchers feeding, or he'd comment on the hideous din of a rookery above them and the sinister shapes of the birds that they'd disturbed. He knew where to look out for pheasant and woodcock and wild duck and wood pigeon and he taught Celia how to spot them. Sometimes one of the setters, who always accompanied them around the roads, would rush up a mountainy field and stop dead still, pointing a bird or a hare. Jimmy always noticed what was happening and they'd rein in the horses to stand and watch.

Whenever the tide was low at the right time Jimmy took the horses to Southerly Strand. When the wind was in the south and the tide was ebbing an eerie effect was created at certain points along the shore of Roaring Water Bay. Celia knew that the out-haul was caused by the tide going out, but she had not known that the sound was at its loudest when the tide ebbed against the wind until Jimmy told her. He was also the first person she had come across who seemed to think the out-haul was romantic. Jimmy said that anyone who listened to it for long enough would want to go writing poetry, even himself. Celia was unsure how far he was joking and how far he was serious. It no longer seemed absurd to imagine that this man read, liked or even wrote poems.

One evening he asked Celia up to his house for a fry after which she was to give him a hand to repair some tack. While they worked with goose grease, strong needles and bradawls Celia asked Jimmy about his stay in London. She was horrified to discover that he'd spent twelve years working in the city as an accountant. She said that for someone like Jimmy to be confined in a stuffy urban place for hours, days, weeks on end, must have been *torture*.

Jimmy was amused at her indignation. It hadn't been that bad at the time – he hadn't allowed it to be. He had taken the opportunity to indulge his liking for fast cars and flashy nightclubs and one-night stands and get it all out of his system as quickly as possible. Through various rackets on the side, some of which he tried to explain to Celia, he had made a considerable amount of money in addition to the salary paid by his immediate employers, and when the attractions of the 'good life' started to fade, he'd begun to invest his money back in Cork. He bought a house in Cork city which he'd converted into apartments, and three properties and a bit of land in the Bally C area. Eventually he got the chance to buy his way into an accountancy firm which became his ticket home, and allowed him to spend as much time as possible on his hobby of training and riding point-to-point horses. One day, he hoped, he would manage to make a living out of the horses. Meanwhile he ran an accountancy firm on his own in Skibbereen to which he dedicated as little time as possible. He was his own boss, and he had managed to retire from the rat race and indulge his own interests by the age of thirty-six. He did not think that twelve years working in the city was such a high price to pay.

The boreen-repairing operation was carried out with Jimmy's usual quiet efficiency. At Ardbeigh, above Southerly Strand, they shovelled stones and gravel into the trailer, with Jimmy loading at about four times the rate that Celia could manage. Then she drove the Land Rover slowly up the boreen, responding to Jimmy's shouts as he shovelled gravel and stones out into the pot holes. After two trips the task was completed. Jimmy said it was only makeshift and it wouldn't last the winter, but they felt pleased enough with themselves to agree that it was worth a small celebration over a glass of shandy in Lily's.

Ben was sitting up at the front bench with Clarissa, both of them staring listlessly at the *Examiner* crossword.

'It's a bastard today,' Ben said to Celia as she walked in the door.

'Absolutely impossible,' said Clarissa. 'Seven across, '*man of the match*', ten letters.'

'Bridegroom,' said Jimmy who was following close behind Celia.

'Good Lord! Maybe he's right,' said Clarissa. 'Let's see . . . one down, '*French author found in stupor*' . . .'

'Proust!' shouted Ben. 'It has to be, it's an anagram of stupor!'

'How bizarre,' said Clarissa. 'How beautifully apt.'

Jimmy and Celia took their drinks over to a side table.

'It's a great feeling to have a day's work done by midday,' said Jimmy.

Celia agreed. She had fed and exercised two horses, mucked out two loose boxes, breakfasted with Jimmy and Con and repaired a boreen and it was still only twelve thirty. She and Jimmy were covered in dust from the gravel, and, though they were unaware of it, carried a strong smell of horse into Lily's with them.

'So how's the gee-gees going?' asked Clarissa.

'Like lightning,' said Jimmy.

Celia laughed, and then said to Jimmy, 'But seriously, the new bay's coming along well, isn't she?'

'She's doing grand. I'm thinking of sending her up to Mallow for some schooling.' Jimmy's uncle trained and bred horses on a stud farm to the north of Cork city and Jimmy often took advantage of the superior facilities of the Mallow establishment. 'You're coming on well too,' he added. 'It's been a long time now since the Strand's run away with you.'

'Touch wood,' said Celia.

'Maybe those days are over.'

'Let's hope so.' Celia got up to fetch another drink. 'We should have had a pint. It's thirsty work, road repairing.'

'Sit down now. I'll get these.' Celia was surprised. She and Jimmy usually observed the alternate round system with great precision. She was even more surprised by his next remark as he set the two pints on the table.

'How would you like a bit of a treat tonight?'

'What?'

'I've a pheasant back at home, just ready for roasting. If I drop it in to you after lunch we could eat it this evening down at your place.'

'Great!'

'You'd be doing me a favour. I don't mind shooting them and plucking them and drawing them, but when it comes to cooking them for one . . .'

'I love cooking.'

'I know. I'll bring a bottle of wine back from Skib and we'll make a real feast of it.'

It was the first time that Celia had entertained anyone to more than a cup of tea and a biscuit in her house, and the first bottle of wine that she'd had on her table since arriving. Jimmy carved the pheasant, and Celia served potatoes and cabbage and mashed turnips on to the best plates.

Jimmy's two setters, Daisy and Duke, had made themselves at home on the familiar hearth rug in front of the wood burner and slept and grunted while Celia and Jimmy ate. The presence of a guest made Celia's house feel very different: more like home.

Jimmy helped Celia to carry the dishes in to the kitchen, then sat back in one of the fireside chairs. There was still half a bottle of wine left and he handed Celia a glass as she sat down in the opposite chair.

‘An excellent meal if I may say so. We must do this more often.’

‘Oh aye.’ Celia sat on the edge of her armchair.

‘Don’t you ever get lonely for all your friends in London,’ said Jimmy. ‘All the cinemas and nightclubs and restaurants?’

‘No, not really. I lived very quietly when I was there. Pretty boring. And I’ve always hated nightclubs.’

‘What about your boyfriend? The one who came over with you last August?’

‘Uuuuf.’ Celia dismissed Nick with a wave of her arm, a gesture she had picked up from Emily. ‘What about you? Don’t you find it very quiet here sometimes?’

Jimmy laughed, ‘And me with three horses, two dogs, four properties and the accountancy business? And twenty acres of oats above in Bawnavota?’

‘I didn’t know about the oats.’

‘Keep it under your hat so,’ said Jimmy and he raised his eyebrows as he stretched his feet out closer to the wood burner.

There was something unusual about the way that Jimmy was looking at Celia, something that excited her. As she stared at his strong compact body sprawled out in the chair, and noticed how sardonic his features became when he arched his eyebrows, she remembered his nickname, the half-sir. Indoors it suited him in a different way. In this relaxed and idle state, a most unusual one for Jimmy, there was something arrogant and aristocratic about him. In London, she reflected, he must have had women falling over him, and she wondered why he had not yet found a replacement for Susan Macarthy.

Celia had never seen Jimmy so dressed up before, not even for Ben’s birthday party on the night of her arrival, and that was another reason why she stared. Tonight, instead of looking like a hard-working stable lad, he could be mistaken for a professional townie on a country weekend.

He'd had a bath and washed his hair and wore a clean shirt and highly polished brogues. His trousers had not a speck of mud on them, and his tweed jacket, though well-worn, was equally spotless.

This careful transformation gave Celia only one idea: that tonight he intended to make a pass at her. It was an idea that she liked.

Jimmy looked her in the eye. 'You must come up to my place one night and watch some videos. I get them from a club up in Cork.'

Celia had expected a line, but not a sleazy one like this.

'*Great Moments in Racing*, you'd enjoy that one, and *The Gay Future Caper*, I bet you've never seen it. It's a documentary about a betting racket.'

She smiled. 'No, I haven't.'

Jimmy looked over at the dresser on which the old television sat.

'There's nothing on the aul box tonight.'

'As usual.'

'So I guess we'll have to make our own entertainment.'

He sat up and reached into the inside pocket of his jacket where he had stored three tin whistles. He selected one and blew a note on it.

'Do you play anything yourself?'

Celia shook her head. The dogs stirred, turning over with a sigh as Jimmy began to play a slow sad air. Celia relaxed back into her chair and closed her eyes in a semi-trance. She wished that the low plaintive notes would never stop twining around her senses, carrying her off to other times and places while making the present time and place almost unbearably vivid . . . her hearth, the dogs sighing and Jimmy playing for her . . .

'But don't stop. It's beautiful.'

Another even more melancholy slow air, then a pretty transition and Celia opened her eyes to the intricate notes of a witty jig. She started tapping with one foot, following

Jimmy's lead as he stood up to catch his breath. He blew a long final note and flourished the tin whistle saying:

'The spoons! We'll get you on the spoons!'

Jimmy bent a pair of spoons, which were, after all, his own, to the correct angle and Celia quickly picked up the knack, even to the point of taking off on improvised solos.

'You're very handy on the spoons,' said Jimmy, taking a breather.

'Nothing to it!'

'What are you planning to do for Lily's cabaret?'

'I've been racking my brains. I'd love to do something, but there's nothing I'm any good at.'

'I'd say the spoons would go down great.'

'Can I really?'

'But a'course. We'll need a few more sessions and then we'll fix a little programme.'

'That's great Jimmy, thanks a million.'

He shook the tin whistle and put it back in his pocket.

'I'd say there's a lot of things we could enjoy together.'

Here it comes, thought Celia, and tried to look demure.

'You must get lonely down here on your own. And there's me on my own up at Bawnavota. Two grown adults. Couldn't you use a bit of company from time to time?'

'Oh aye.' Breathless and almost whispering.

Jimmy took her hand. 'Nothing more. Just a bit of company, a nice warm body in the bed on a cold winter night.'

Celia nodded.

'You remember what I told you about not making pets of horses? Not getting too fond of them?'

She'd been warned that the animals had to earn their keep. Lameness, broken wind, going sour, any serious loss of form would mean the knackers. Sentimental attachments were to be avoided.

'I'm a bit like that myself. I'm not the person you should go getting fond of. I've no mind to marry and I've no mind to fall in love. If this is going to spoil our friendship then I'd rather just have the friendship.'

'Don't worry. As you say, just a bit of company.'

'That's the girl! You've grand spirit.' And he led her upstairs to bed.

Jimmy, as her landlord, had a key to Celia's house, but he never used it to let himself in. Their relationship when working the horses remained unchanged, except that sometimes, over breakfast at Con's, Jimmy would rub his stockinged foot against Celia's under the table and look approvingly at her across it.

For the first week they slept together every night except for the Sunday. Jimmy was leaving for Cork at six o'clock on Monday morning and had business to look over beforehand.

She became equally at home in his house or hers. His house had the advantage of the video and the colour television, but hers was warmer. He had the better kitchen, but she had the better food. Jimmy appeared to live on the frying pan: sausages, rashers, black and white pudding, eggs, and doorsteps of white bread.

Jimmy often had to see clients in the evenings, and he had committee meetings of the local hunt. Three times a week he drove Con down to Lily's. Celia let him know that his knock would be welcome on the door at any time, but he seldom called on her after eleven, insisting that they both needed a few good nights' sleep a week to keep some of their energy for working the horses. Eventually they settled into a pattern of sleeping together on more-or-less alternate nights.

It was not enough for Celia. At first she thought maybe she enjoyed sex with Jimmy so much because it had been a while – Nick – since she'd had any. But by the third night she knew it was more than that. Jimmy was the closest she had ever come to finding perfect physical compatibility.

She had never been so blatantly eager for any man. And the more she had him, the more she wanted him.

He was a straightforward lover, sensual and considerate. When they were joined together and moving in harmony he always asked:

'Nice?'

'Nice?'

'Nice?'

which aroused Celia to even greater heights, and with her hands kneading the firm muscles of his back and shoulders she would feel deep waves of warmth and pleasure.

'Nice?'

'Nice?'

'Nice?'

as she started to come

'Nice?'

and came

'Nice?'

'Nice?'

'aaaah!'

'aaaaaah!'

'ah'

'ah . . .'

'mmmmmmm'

'uuuuf'

xxx

He always kissed her afterwards, gently, on her cheek or on the side of her neck, then they rolled apart and lay on their backs holding hands and drifted off into a deep restful sleep.

Celia was a woman of her word, and she did her best to avoid falling in love with Jimmy. She often reminded herself that to have good sex with a good friend when there are no other emotional attachments in your life can engender all kinds of delusions. Just because she liked Jimmy and they got on well in bed and out of it, it did not necessarily have to follow that they would fall in love. But if Jimmy were ever to give her the slightest encouragement, Celia would be only too ready to admit that she now felt for him something far more passionate and obsessive than the usual affection found in a friendship.

DECEMBER

Ben and Clarissa were huddled together at a side table in Lily's recovering from their weekend shopping. Clarissa was highly animated.

'She's having it off with the half-sir. Absolutely no doubt about it. His jeep was down there all night *again*. Third time in a week.'

'So what?'

'So you've left it too bloody late. Five to one they move in together before Christmas.'

'Five blow-jobs to one?'

'Hah! You'd be lucky.' Clarissa took a long drink from her pint of lager.

'Yeah. I'm damn lucky if I see any action at all these days.'

'Well, that's your fault, isn't it? You're such a slow mover. I've had the fat lady lined up for weeks and you haven't lifted a finger.'

'I'm going shooting with the half-sir this evening. I'll make a few discreet enquiries.'

'Discreet enquiries!' Clarissa turned away in disgust. What was the point of having an open relationship when the other partner never got up to anything? Ben did not, of course, know about *all* of Clarissa's adventures. He preferred to turn a blind eye to her mysterious absences and believe the excuses she presented, which usually involved her need to be alone to think about her work.

Clarissa was finding their 'open relationship' a very enjoyable one. But Ben, beyond announcing that he fancied

Celia, appeared to have remained inactive.

Clarissa was getting impatient. 'Okay,' she said, 'five blow-jobs to one if you fuck her before midnight.'

'Tomorrow,' said Ben. 'I told you, I'm going shooting with Jimmy this evening and I don't want to stand him up. He's promised me a loan of Duke and I could use a good dog . . .'

'Where are you meeting him?'

'In here at half five.'

'I'll be here. I'll give him some excuse.'

Ben thought again about Celia's fleshy curves and her easy-going smile.

'Five to one?'

'Five to one.'

He stood up to leave.

'Hang on. I've got to get the shopping home and you said you'd chop some kindling . . .'

'Tough titty sweetheart.' And Ben waved five fingers at Clarissa as he left Lily's.

Ben blinked at the grey light in the street. His head hurt. Goddamn poitín the night before. There was no hangover on earth could compare . . .

He turned the corner towards Celia's house, pulled his shoulders back, and forced a cheerful expression on to his face. He knocked on Celia's door.

'Ben! Come on in . . .'

Celia chattered. Horses, mares, bitches, setters, pasties, Jimmy, Skibbereen, Emily, Edward, Aoife, Mrs Harte, cup of tea . . . A banal pop song was blaring from the radio. The shabby pink and turquoise room oppressed Ben.

'I'll drive you to Skib.'

'Right now?'

'Sure. With the pasties. Let's make a day of it.'

The tray of pasties on the back seat filled the car with a

warm smell of food that turned Ben's stomach. A glass of Paddy in Cotters while Celia delivered her wares to the delicatessen restored him, and confirmed his intention.

'Where to now?' She was at his elbow, smiling like a twelve-year-old.

Ben did his best to look and sound amiably conspiratorial: 'We'll take ourselves off on a spree! Are you on?'

'Why not?' Anything for a change. Celia followed Ben out of Cotters to his car.

He took her to a gloomy bar in a small fishing village to the east of Skibbereen. One of Clarissa's favourite haunts.

As they entered the empty room the man behind the bar looked up from the newspaper and asked:

'Do you know that we are subsisting in an EEC Peripheral Maritime Zone?'

'Good on ya, Dominic,' said Ben. 'Meet Celia.'

Celia and Dominic shook hands. Dominic was a black-haired man about Jimmy's age, with a devious smile. Celia liked the look of him.

'How's Clarissa?' he asked.

'Same as ever. Sends her love,' said Ben, suspecting that this was a deliberate attempt by Dominic to embarrass Celia and put him on the hot spot. The fact that it didn't made Ben feel a bit flat.

'Sit up here and tell me all the news from Bally C,' said Dominic. 'How's the company in Lily's?'

Celia and Ben sat for two hours drinking bloody Marys and exchanging gossip with Dominic. It was Celia who kept the conversation going, responding immediately to Dominic's lively charm. He reminded her a little of Jimmy, but Dominic told a much better story, elaborating on the simplest local occurrence to make it seem worthy of coverage in the international press.

While Celia and Dominic became more lively with every drink, Ben appeared to be sliding into an increasingly morose state. They were the only people in Dominic's bar that afternoon, and Dominic was determined to coax Ben back on to form.

Dominic looked at the bar counter that lay between himself and his customers.

'Ben. Would you tell me why there are four empty glasses on that bar?' he asked.

Ben came alive.

'You're wrong Dominic. There's only three. Yours, mine and Celia's.'

'I tell you there are four. I can see four empty glasses on that bar.' He paused, then looked at Celia. 'How many do you see?'

'Three,' said Celia. 'Definitely three glasses.'

'I see four.'

'Three,' said Ben. Then he got suspicious. What the hell was Dominic trying to say? 'How come you see four?'

'I see four.'

Dominic was a sly one. A great favourite of Clarissa's. Ben was determined to get to the bottom of it. 'Tell me, how come you see four glasses on that bar?'

Dominic spoke slowly. 'I see four. If I'm wrong, will you buy me a drink?'

'You're on.'

'I'm wrong so! There's only *three* glasses there, and you owe me a bloody Mary . . .'

Hook, line and sinker. Ben left his loose change and a note on the bar counter and escorted Celia out of the door before she and Dominic had stopped laughing.

From Dominic's the quality of bar and bar person went steadily downhill, and so did Ben. By the time they walked into the third cold empty stone-floored bar and took seats at the remotest corner table in silence, Celia had had enough.

'Ben?'

'Uh?'

'What's up with you today? I thought we were supposed to be having fun, taking a spree . . . are you worried about something?'

'Hell, Celia. I'm sorry. I guess Dominic kinda rubbed me up the wrong way.'

'What, with that stupid old joke?'

'No, not that . . . I guess he started me thinking about Clarissa, and I kinda wanted to get away from that.'

'Are things a bit, you know . . .?'

Hell. So gauche. Why couldn't she just come out with it? But then he wasn't being much better himself. He tried to take a hold of the conversation.

'Clarissa thinks I've taken you out to seduce you.'

Celia collapsed in laughter. Ben felt offended. Surely the idea was not that comical.

'I bet that's not how *she* put it!' said Celia when she was able. 'Jesus, that woman has a one-track mind if ever I met one. Can't two people just be friends without leaping into bed?' And she was off again, laughing.

This was not how things were supposed to turn out, but Ben didn't care. Clarissa's knowledge of his intentions had taken all the fun out of the idea of fucking Celia. And he had started to see her as someone remarkably ordinary, not even the fleshy curves and the smile . . . she was too goddamn sane and straightforward for this kind of scene.

'Yeah, goddamn crazy idea,' he said, with something closer to his usual gusto. 'Let's just go right ahead and have ourselves a good time. A *real* good time!'

They made their way slowly back towards Bally C, stopping at every bar on the road. In spite of Ben's efforts to be jovial, it was not really much of a spree as sprees go, and like many sprees, it ended up in a ditch.

Celia later tried to remember how many bars they visited, but lost count after the first seven. After Dominic's, Ben did not seem to get any drunker, but he seldom showed evidence of having taken drink until he passed out. Besides paying for all the drinks, he also insisted on doing all the driving, so Celia allowed herself to become extremely drunk. As Ben kept telling her, the occasional binge was a necesssary antidote to the quiet routine of their existence in Bally C.

They hit the ditch quite slowly on a bad bend about five miles outside Bally C. Both could see the road coming up to meet them in the headlights, grass verge, not tarmac, and Ben braked gently as the front wheel slid into the dyke and sank. They were on the wrong side of the road too, though neither of them knew why, so that when Ben climbed out of his door he landed up to his ankles in muddy water. The shock caused him to drop the car keys which he had automatically removed from the ignition. By the time that Celia had climbed uphill out of the passenger door and made her way across the front of the car to give Ben a hand, they were both helpless with laughter. Ben somehow got himself back on to dry land and leant on Celia's shoulders as they stumbled around the middle of the road, pausing occasionally to catch their breath and point at the car and start laughing again.

'Where the hell are we?'

'The car's headed that way so that must be the way to Bally C.'

'Don't count on it.'

And off again.

They needed to lean on each other to walk. Ben had lost a shoe in the ditch as well as his keys so he took off the other shoe and threw it over a hedge. His main worry was whether they would make it to Lily's by closing time.

'I can hear the old bat already: "the state of you!" *Ha!* Just let her try to refuse me a hot whiskey . . .'

It was a cold moonless night with a clinging damp in the air. Celia was glad she was not alone. She always carried a strong flashlight in her car and wished that Ben had taken the same precaution. She did not like the dark. Without him she would have been terrified. It was an irrational fear: she knew that the small animals in the ditches were only rats and voles and field mice who would never harm her, but still they made her nervous. The absence of traffic was eerie, and the night was so dense and they were so drunk that it was not easy to keep to the side of the road and she often found herself tripping over invisible cat's eyes.

Ben stopped and turned to Celia, trying to look into her eyes in the darkness.

'Do you know something Celia?'

'– ?'

'Suddenly it don't seem so crazy after all. The idea of you and me fucking . . .'

One passionate kiss. Then Celia, confused, but also a little flattered, unwrapped herself from his arms.

'Don't do that. I need you to lean on.'

'There's a car coming.'

Celia crossed the road, turned to face the traffic and stuck her thumb out.

It was Boris in his Merc. They both got into the back seat and Celia pulled the door shut.

Boris was listening to *Der Freischütz* at full blast on his car stereo. He showed no interest at all in why Ben and Celia were hitching a lift in the middle of nowhere, but continued to sing along with the music as the car sped through the black night. Unlike Boris, Ben and Celia did not know the words, but soon found the temptation to join in irresistible.

It was a tape of operatic greatest hits, and when the Chorus of the Huntsman was followed by the drinking song from La Traviata the three of them stayed in the car singing, even though they were by then parked outside Lily's.

Christmas promotions began early in Bally C that year. Fairy lights went up in most of the bar and shop windows and the district council strung a few more over the ruined castle. Connolly's, the supermarket, replaced the usual musical sludge – which their customers had more or less learnt to put up with – by a strident American compilation of carols.

Ian took such exception to a little song with the chorus:

Deck the halls with boughs of holly
Tra la la la la la-la la-la
'Tis the season to be jolly
Tra la la la la la-la la-la

that every time it came round he would dump his metal basket on the floor and block his ears with his fists.

This was the posture in which Celia found him on the Saturday after her spree. She had managed to struggle from her bed to ride out with Jimmy and bake a batch of pasties for Lily, but had then fallen asleep in an armchair and woken up just in time to dash over to Connolly's before they closed.

'I'm not sure I can stand it,' said Ian loudly, his hands still over his ears. 'We've got to put up with this racket until the sixth of bloody January.'

'Go on, Ian, where's your Christmas spirit?'

'You can talk! Been in any good ditches lately?'

Celia blushed, 'Oh, don't! My head!'

'You were well away last night! Bloody flying. I've just got in from giving Ben a tow back on to the road. You're lucky he was going so slowly or it could have been right messy.'

'I can't remember a thing after drinking hot whiskeys in Lily's. God knows how I got myself home and into bed. Is the car all right?'

'Yeah. The wing was a bit bent but I unbent it. It's just as well you left Lily's before old Ben passed out. Me and Boris had to carry him into the Merc and drive him up to

Clarissa. She was like a *bear* . . . Hey up! Speak a' the devil.'

Ben was stocking up on Camels at the check-out. He waved sheepishly at Celia then disappeared into the darkness outside.

He was still waiting there when Celia came out with her shopping and startled her by sliding out of the shadows.

'Hi there.'

'Ben!'

'Wanna drink? Just a quick one?'

'No, I couldn't, I really couldn't . . .'

'Hair of the dog. One therapeutic bloody Mary.'

'Oh, all right. But then I have to get an early night.'

Ben led her up the hill to the hotel.

'You don't mind, do you? I wanted somewhere quiet.'

'This is fine.'

The hotel bar was deserted as usual. They rang the bell on the counter for Dermot. He served them in silence then disappeared.

'Ian told me the car's okay.'

'Yeah. And the keys were on the floor. That was a stroke of luck. He's a good guy, Ian. I'll be sorry to see him go.'

'Where's he going?'

'England. He's flat broke, can't afford to re-tax the van and insure it so he's selling it to some friend up in Cork and getting on the ferry.'

'That's a shame! What about the goats and *Château Despair?*'

'Oh, he'll be back. Emily's going to take the goats, and the trailer can stay where it is. He'll probably turn up again at Easter.'

They were silent for a few minutes. Ben shifted in his chair.

'Uh, Celia?'

'What?'

'I hope you're not sore about yesterday?'

'Sore? No, it was great fun. The whole day was.'

'Look, I did something kinda dumb this morning. But if I can square it with you, you'd be doing me a great favour . . .'

'What?' Celia was lost.

'Clarissa thinks I screwed you yesterday, and she's delighted. Just a misunderstanding, but it would make life a hell of a lot easier for me if I could let her go on believing that. Just to keep her quiet.'

'I don't understand . . . what do you mean?'

'She wants to believe that I'm having an affair, and if she thinks I'm having one with you, then that lets me off the hook . . . she'll stop bugging me about it . . . see what I mean?'

'Sort of.'

'Look, I didn't even need to tell you this. I'm asking your permission because you're a friend, because I like you, and I don't want to mess you around. Clarissa won't go boasting about it to anyone, and neither will I. No one has to know beyond the three of us. And once Clarissa calms down we can break it off . . .'

'Ben, that's ridiculous, why on earth . . .'

'Please?' Ben could be very charming when he wanted to, and Celia was feeling somewhat below par.

'Supposing Jimmy heard about it?'

'He won't. I promise you that. No one will hear about it.'

Celia was tempted. After all, she and Jimmy were merely friends and lovers. He had never demanded anything of her beyond friendship and sex. He had been amused, not jealous at the story of her spree. For all she knew he might have other women up in Cork, and he probably didn't give a damn about her faithfulness or lack of it. Anyway, she could always explain . . .

It was the same confusion and flattery she had felt at Ben's sudden kiss the night before. Her morale was lifted by the notion that Ben, who was, in spite of his many faults, a published writer, and therefore rather special in Celia's eyes, could show an interest in someone so ordinary as her. This would make the two of them conspirators in a game that excluded even the almighty Clarissa . . .

'Okay then. But your absolute word of honour that we'll break it off as soon as we can . . .'

Ben laughed. 'You're dynamite, kid.'

The next time they saw each other was at the meeting of the Cabaret Committee, a body invented by Boris. He had pinned a notice up in Lily's announcing the meeting, and then informed all those who intended to perform in the cabaret that they were honorary committee members and therefore under strict obligation to attend the preliminary meeting.

It was held in Lily's back room, and Boris had drawn up an agenda which he read out to the assembled company:

1. Date of Cabaret.
2. Description of acts and running length.
3. Order of performance.
4. Installation of sound system and other technical problems.
5. Dress.
6. Rehearsal schedule.

'Hang about,' said Ian, 'We don't need all that crap. Christmas Eve, nine o'clock, everyone does their act and brings some nosh and we all wear what the hell we like. End of meeting. Let's play poker.'

'I second that!' shouted Ben.

'Shut up,' said Clarissa. 'Boris is right, it was an absolute shambles last year. If we're going to do it at all, we should do it properly.'

'I suggest we move it from Christmas Eve to the Saturday

before Christmas,' said Emily. 'Just for once in my life I'd like to start Christmas Day without a hangover.'

There was general agreement to Emily's suggestion and Boris's pocket diary was consulted.

'Will Susan be home by then?' Charlie asked Daniel.

'Oh aye. And Morty.'

'Saturday the nineteenth so,' said Boris. 'Agreed?'

'Agreed.'

'Descriptions of acts and running length,' Boris read from his agenda. 'We go round the room clockwise from my right. Ian.'

'Me and Ben's playing blues guitar.'

'Jazz guitar,' said Ben.

'Jazz blues,' said Ian.

'Celia?'

'I'm doing an act with Jimmy.'

Clarissa burst into loud laughter, and so did Emily and Daniel. The meeting disintegrated in vulgar mirth. When Celia, who had simply been trying to avoid saying 'spoons' saw that Jimmy was laughing as loudly as anyone, she had to join in. She even found that she enjoyed this friendly recognition of her relationship to Jimmy.

Order was restored, and Boris completed his list: Emily – Belly Dance, The Macarthys – string band, Clarissa – verse reading, and himself – operatic interlude, with each act limited to a maximum of ten minutes in length. Emily and Boris needed a cassette player to provide musical backing, and after some discussion they were grouped together either side of the interval, and he had a running order written down:

Tin whistle and spoons
String band
Belly dance
Interval

Operatic interlude
Verse reading
Jazz blues guitars

The guitars were then supposed to be joined by Jimmy and the Macarthys to transform the cabaret into a session featuring Con's gadget, Barney Mack's rebel songs, Lily's party piece and anything else that was offered by the company.

Boris did not get far with the rest of his agenda. Jimmy, Ian, Ben and the Macarthys all refused to wear dinner jackets for the very good reason that they did not own one. No one wanted a run-through as it would take away from their enjoyment of the acts on the night, and no one wanted to hear what food other people were bringing for the same reason. Nevertheless, Boris was reasonably satisifed that some sort of order had been imposed on the chaos.

Emily turned the Morris into the airport approach road, greatly relieved to have made the journey from Bally C without a breakdown and in just under two hours.

Aoife and Edward came alive in the back seat.

'Mummy, mummy, we're here mummy!'

'I know, I know.'

'Can I put the coin in the slot mummy?'

'No, Edward, you do that when you *leave* the car park. You can do it when you come back.'

'Can we have a snack, mummy?'

'You can a'course.'

They were one hour early for the flight: Emily's insurance against foul weather, punctures and other delays. Aoife ran ahead into the terminal building and came back with a baggage trolley.

As Emily pushed it through the doors Edward stopped to talk to the security guard at the entrance checkpoint.

'Ttttell me, do you ccccatch many ttttterrorists here?'

Emily's ex-husband, David, had made an appointment for Edward with a speech therapist in London. And he had tickets for the *Nutcracker* at the Festival Hall. Grandma was playing hostess and Santa Claus for three whole weeks. No doubt the children would have a whale of a time.

Emily cringed at the artificial brightness of the worn green carpet as she followed the children upstairs, carrying their boarding passes in her left hand. In her memory the airport was a special place for emotional partings and reunions, and she was always slightly shocked when she had time enough to notice its gaudy shabbiness. The children never failed to find it thrilling.

Aoife turned to Emily and pointed at a plate of garishly decorated trifle. 'Can I have one of those mummy?' she asked doubtfully.

Emily felt a pang at this reminder of her habitual strictness with the children. Her firmness on their shopping trips to Bantry and Skibbereen was needed in order to ensure that they lived within their means, but she tempered it by well-reasoned explanations about the stupidity and waste of eating out when they had a farm-full of superior produce at home.

'You can a'course, love. Have whatever you want. You too, Edward, don't you want a trifle as well?'

Emily took a cup of coffee for herself and they sat at a round table in the middle of the deserted concourse at the top of the stairs. She wished that the children would stop looking at her as if she'd gone mad. Couldn't they understand that this was different? It was the transition from her form of care to that of their father and grandmother. It was a limbo where everything was allowed. Then Emily heard her husband's sarcastic tones, the words he would surely be speaking before the day was out? 'Really? Mummy let you have a *whole* plate of trifle *each* at the airport? How super of mummy, how absolutely thrilling . . .'

Edward cut in on her reverie: 'It's not really very nice. It only looks nice. It's not as nice as your tttttrifle.'

Must not cry. She stirred her coffee and watched Edward watching her. Emily battled against it constantly, but there was no way to fool her conscience. Edward was her favourite child. There was something uncanny about the way that he understood her and intuitively expressed his understanding when she needed support. Aoife was wonderful, but so obviously beautiful, talented, competent and well-balanced that she had already learnt to lead her own life without needing any special rapport with her mother. She needed approval and encouragement, the usual reassurances that any girl of eleven needs, then she went off again along her own remarkably self-sufficient path. Emily was proud of Aoife, but Aoife's perfection never moved her in the way that Edward's strangeness did.

Three weeks without them – she knew the pattern already, the initial sense of loss, then a self-indulgently disorganised timetable and a bout of gregariousness and alcoholic excess, then, just as she'd got used to being on her own, it would be back to the airport and weeks on end of 'grandma says and daddy says and in London we always did, why can't we here . . .' until the normal regime was re-established.

Oh well.

A gin and tonic was called for.

Hang about, as Ian would say. It was just on eleven a.m. . . . 'and then mummy went to the bar and she had two gin and tonics and we had a red lemonade each . . .'

What the hell. Emily reminded herself that she was, after all, a grown up (and normally quite an abstemious one by Bally C standards) and, as such, if she felt like having a gin and tonic or two at eleven a.m. on a Thursday, she would do so. And if the children threw up all over their father on arrival at Heathrow, so be it. Give him a chance to wipe up the puke for a change.

He'd probably think she'd gone bonkers anyway. This time she hadn't even bothered to pack a supply of new clothes for the children, knowing that their grandma always replaced her home-made and Bantry-bought items with stuff from Harrods. Emily had stopped trying to make her mother-in-law appreciate how well she looked after the children. Their values were too disparate. If their wealthy, fashionable grandmother thought Emily gave the children a tough time, so what?

They moved to the bar.

Edward unpacked a puzzle book from his satchel which was supposed to keep him amused on the plane. Aoife was filling it in at a rate of knots, allowing no time for her younger brother to follow the solutions. Emily came back with the drinks and called a halt.

'Let's play battleships.' She so seldom seemed to have time to play with the children, however hard she tried to make sure that she did. They were delighted. Aoife had Edward and Emily beaten from the start, but they played on in noisy good humour, and if it hadn't been for Aoife's sharp hearing, she and Edward might have missed the flight altogether.

'Nice?'

'Nice?'

'Nice?'

'mmm.'

'Nice?'

'ah!'

'uf'

'mmm'

xxx

Silence and darkness.

'Jimmy?'

'Mmmm?'

'Jimmy . . . do you mind if I ask you something?'

'Mm?'

'Is it all right if I can get a little bit fond of you? More than I would of someone who was just a friend? Can I do that?'

'You can a'course Celia.'

zzzzzzzzzzz

Ian was walking up the road in the rain carrying his guitar case. His hair was soaked already, only a few hundred yards from *Château Despair*, and drops were falling down the neck of his leather jacket. He'd forgotten his neckscarf and his woolly hat. It was a heavy grey downpour that showed no signs of easing.

He saw a figure in yellow oilskins on the road ahead of him and gave a shout: 'Hey up! Celia!'

She stopped and waited as he caught up with her, then she greeted him: 'Filthy isn't it? Where are you off to?'

'Well, I was planning to go busking outside the post office for the price of a stamp, but with this weather . . .'

'Ian! I can give you a stamp. D'you want the loan of a fiver?'

'No, I was only kidding, luv. I'm on my way up to Ben's for a rehearsal.'

'Got time for a quick drink first? I'm buying.'

'Yer on.'

Lily commiserated with them on their wetness and lent Ian a towel to dry his hair. She then gave him a white plastic bag and instructions to wear it on his head on his way up to Ben's. He protested, she insisted:

'I've precious few customers this time of year and I can't afford to go losing one through the pneumonia . . .'

Once Lily had left them alone Ian said, 'I will have that stamp if you don't mind. Have you got it on you?'

Celia handed it over and Ian stuck it on a small brown envelope.

'Herein lies the solution to all my problems,' he said.

Celia took it from him. It was addressed to a biscuit manufacturing company in Dublin and was still unsealed.

'Tell me more.'

'Yeah, maybe I can pick your brains. Three end papers from your favourite super-saver biscuits, and complete the slogan 'Tea's not tea without – blank –' in my case, custard creams.'

'Go on.'

'First prize a holiday for two in New York or £2500 cash equivalent. And £3000 worth of consolation prizes.'

'And the slogan?'

Ian paused. 'It looks better written down.'

'Go on.'

'Tea's not tea without custard creams
Because custard creams are the stuff of dreams.'

He looked embarrassed: 'Well, Clarissa helped. I thought it should have been the food of dreams, or the snack of dreams, but she says 'stuff'. Says it's better. What d'you reckon?'

Celia muttered the slogan under breath with all three alternatives, and tried to imagine the judges at the biscuit company listening to her.

'Not snack, and food's a bit much. No, I think Clarissa's right, "stuff". Good luck!'

'Here's to the end of poverty!'

They took a sip of beer.

'Are things really that bad? Ben told me you're going back to England.'

'Not if my custard creams come through, I'm not. Otherwise, yeah. Got to flog the fucking van and I can't work here without the van, even if I had any work.'

'I'm sorry.'

'Oh, it's just one of those things, you know. It happens, and you come through it. I just want to work, self-respect and that sort of thing, feel a bit of money in my pocket for once. I've had it with knitting bloody socks and signing on. I'm a good tradesman and the brother's got this business doing flat conversions in Hendon and he reckons I can pick up a few bob, then I'll come back around Easter. Maybe.'

Ian sounded very gloomy, but he cheered up: 'I phoned the brother reverse charges last night. Know what he said?'

'No.' (A' course not.)

'That I mustn't think of it as poverty. I'm broke, and that's different. Poverty's like no way out of it, you are bloody lumbered. Broke is a temporary state of affairs – that's how he talks, the brother – a temporary state of affairs, usually self-imposed. Geddit?'

Celia thought.

'Like if I choose to stay on in Bally C, I'll go on being broke, right? At least until the summer. But if I go back to Hendon, just for a couple of months even, I can get a few quid together and come back to Bally C with some cash. So that's not being poor, it's being broke.'

'Yes. It makes sense.' Celia could see the parallels to her own situation. 'It's so awful having to leave when you don't want to. When are you off?'

'I'm getting the ferry on the twenty-eighth so I'll be around for Christmas.'

'I know. We're both going up to Emily.'

'And I'll be back as soon as I bloody well can.'

Lily always dressed up for the cabaret – her best green velvet. It was only fair, she thought, given the effort that everyone put into it. And she had Pake in to help behind the bar because the cabaret always meant a packed house.

This was the third time that the cabaret had been organised. It had grown out of the spontaneous session that occurred on Christmas Eve which now followed on after the set acts. The cabaret seemed to improve the quality of the session. Lily always enjoyed the Macarthys' act: such a musical family, their father would be proud of the poor creatures. She was not so happy about Clarissa's recitation, but Ben had explained to her that Clarissa only used the bad language because she was a modern poet. That also explained to Lily why Clarissa thought nothing of Barney Mack's lovely long recitations in ballad metre: she was too modern to understand.

Ian and Boris had spent the afternoon setting up the sound system – Boris's cassette player amplified through the speakers of Ben's record player. Then Charlie and Jimmy hung the back room with chains that had been made from red and green paper by Celia and Clarissa. Barney Mack had brought along a cardboard box full of laurel leaves and holly with red berries, and Lily used that to decorate the front bar.

At six o'clock the team gathered at the front bench for the first drink of the evening, before going home to change. Their respective donations of party food had been left in Lily's kitchen. The hard work was over and now there was nothing left to do but enjoy themselves.

Ian walked with Celia to her door. It was a cold, clear night that promised a touch of frost.

'See you at half seven, then. You're sure that's all right, luv?'

'But a'course. I'll try not to use all the water, so you should have enough for a quick dip at least.'

'See you later then.'

Celia went straight into the kitchen and turned the oven on, leaving it, and the bathroom door open. She had long ago given up the habit of a daily bath, which was more of an ordeal than a pleasure, and instead adopted the general Bally C custom of having a daily wash at the basin and waiting until one felt really dirty before bathing. In winter this was seldom more than once a week. Ian borrowed her bathroom once a fortnight, leaving a donation towards the cost of the hot water.

She went back into the front room carrying a bottle of dry sherry and two glasses and opened up the wood burner to warm herself. She had bought another bottle of sherry and two of Rioja to contribute to Christmas Day at Clogheen. But she looked on the cabaret evening as the highlight of her Christmas. She had never been involved in anything quite like it before.

She picked up a letter from her mother which was lying on the chair and contained, thank goodness, a cheque in lieu of a present. She smiled as she re-read the closing sentence of the letter – 'I cannot understand why you insist on living in Bally C and cooking pasties when you could be making a good living anywhere in the world and I only hope that eventually you will get bored enough with the place to come back to civilisation.'

– *Bored* in Bally C? It was inconceivable to Celia.

By the time that Ian arrived carrying his guitar and a plastic bag of clothes, Celia was dressed, made-up and ready. With Emily in her belly-dancing outfit, Celia decided that nothing she chose could be too extravagant, so she wore her only party dress – a low-cut off-the-shoulder one in black moiré with a slit at the side of the skirt.

Ian wolf-whistled, which was the appropriate reaction. Celia had left her hair loose instead of tying it in her usual pony tail, and had gone a bit mad with eyeliner and lip gloss. She knew it was a tarty-looking dress, and always enjoyed the comments provoked by her rare excursions into glamour.

Emily too was enjoying herself up at Clogheen among her little-used pots of kohl and glitter. She'd learnt the art of belly-dancing from a group of Armenian students at university and practised it mainly as a form of relaxation. But now and again she enjoyed indulging a certain exhibitionist streak by dressing up to give a proper show.

Lily allowed Emily the use of one of her bedrooms so that she could save her first entrance for the act. She slipped through the early arrivals and up to her room at half past eight to spend half an hour alone going through her preliminary exercises.

At about the same time, Clarissa was making her final selection of poems. She knew that her reading was far from being the most popular turn in the cabaret, but everyone always insisted that she do it. Why, she could never understand, but she looked on it as practice, keeping her hand in for some future date. However, it annoyed her that she never seemed to make a satisfactory selection of her verse. This year, having just completed the three hundred, she had decided to do something slightly different. The poems were stored numerically in a cardboard box on the floor of her workroom. Inside the files the poems were paper-clipped together in batches of ten. At random she picked one batch of ten from the first hundred, one batch of ten from the second hundred and one batch of ten from the third hundred. She planned to ask Lily to select one from each batch by choosing a number between one and ten. She put the thirty poems into the dark red leather folder which she always carried to readings, and smoothed down the high-necked long black dress which she always wore for readings.

She was ready.

'Hey, who's the sexy broad?' Ben also wolf-whistled as Celia and Ian took off their coats and threw them on the floor behind the back benches.

He gave her a kiss and bought them both a drink. Jimmy, who was down at the other end of the bar with Con and Barney Mack, waved at her and raised his eyebrows.

'Everybody take your seats please. The cabaret will begin in three minutes.' Boris was pushing people into the already packed back room, where Lily had taken the place of honour. Half the clientele of the Penny Farthing seemed to be in Lily's, as well as all her regulars. Some had to stand in the doorway of the back room, and others stood behind them on chairs, looking over their heads.

There was an expectant hush, then a few laughs as Boris, self-appointed compère, stood in the corner set apart as the stage, and searched the room for his opening act.

Celia and Jimmy were standing near the door. Jimmy squeezed her hand. 'You're a picture tonight,' he said. 'Best looking girl in town.'

In response to Boris's frantic wave they began threading their way through the tightly packed crowd. Ben started cheering and applause broke out. As soon as they reached the stage Jimmy gave Celia the one-two-three and they launched straight into their act without the benefit of Boris's introduction. He stood to one side in confusion, then leant against the wall with a shrug, causing a further ripple of laughter.

It was a perfect warm-up act, and by the final number, the whole room was tapping feet and glasses in time to the music. As arranged, Celia and Jimmy took their bow holding hands, smiling at each other and then at the audience. Then, before the applause had died down, Jimmy grabbed her around the waist and gave her a kiss on the mouth. Celia was so taken aback that she kept her eyes wide open, and watched the audience react with delight:

'Good man yerself Jimmy!'

'And again boy!'

'Show her how Jim boy!'

Celia got several friendly slaps on the rump and a wicked pinch from Con as she and Jimmy made their way to their reserved bit of standing space at the side of the room where more drinks had been lined up.

Meanwhile the Macarthys were gathering at the front of the room. Susan and Morty had arrived only that afternoon. It was the first time Celia had seen them, and she stared with curiosity at the woman whom Emily had referred to as 'Jimmy's ex'. Susan was, in Celia's eyes, perfectly exquisite: small and slim with long black hair and a red silk shirt tied stylishly in a knot at the waist of her jeans. She had perfect pale skin and dark blue eyes and when she smiled her two front teeth crossed each other crookedly, destroying the illusion of perfect beauty but adding a far more likeable touch of wit to her face. Celia wondered why on earth Jimmy had not wanted to marry Susan. Now that she had seen her she knew she'd have to ask him. Later that night, she decided, when they were alone.

'Get a bloody move on,' muttered Clarissa, as Marie started tuning her fiddle to Charlie's banjo and Daniel's guitar.

'I love your dress,' said Celia.

'Yours isn't bad either. Wish I had the tits for that sort of thing. Very Renoiresque.'

Celia bristled.

'Oh God, the hunk's back in town,' said Clarissa. 'What an arse!'

'Who? Morty?'

'Yes . . . they're off.'

It was a great act. Daniel and Charlie were working on a fusion of Irish traditional and American blue grass music and had evolved a distinctive style. The audience went wild after the first number and wilder after the second. The act had already run over its allotted ten minutes when they started a third number, and as it ended Boris took the floor in front of the group, and, while pretending to applaud, pointed emphatically at his watch. The Macarthys left the stage and carried their instruments upstairs out of the way.

Celia, Ben, Clarissa and Boris were busy distributing candles to people in the audience to provide suitable lighting for Emily's act. Ian had already put on a tape of Eastern music and lit a dish of incense cones beside the cassette player. He switched off the lights and the room glowed unfamiliar and mysterious in candlelight.

Jimmy was caressing Celia's neck under her loose hair

with one hand. She had an arm around his waist under his jacket and leant back against his shoulder. He kissed the nape of her neck gently and whispered in her ear: 'D'you know, I think I'm getting far too fond of you.'

'Good Lord,' thought Celia, genuinely surprised. 'He's getting romantic at long last. Whatever next?'

Emily's dance was perfection. Given the small space available she concentrated on small movements and simple hand gestures, floating rather than flying. Celia, along with the rest of the audience, was mesmerised as Emily's dancing went gradually faster and faster. She had expected it to be a bit of a laugh, some kind of burlesque. Instead it was not Emily swirling about, but some accomplished eastern stranger, pulling the whole room into her rhythm, quickening the pace, then freezing and starting another slow build up.

Celia whispered in Jimmy's ear – 'She's wonderful.'

'So are you.'

He had decided to take her to Cork for Christmas. First they'd go up to Mallow with the horses, he'd drive Con's box and she could follow with the Land Rover. Then he'd take her to his parents' home for Christmas Day. They'd assume that he was serious about a woman at last, and maybe, at last, he was.

There was a slight pause when Emily ended her dance, squatting on the floor with one leg outstretched, her head on her knee and her hands raised in a gesture of offering. Then applause, during which she made her escape up the back stairs.

Ian reluctantly put on the tape of Christmas carols loaned by Connolly's. He'd been careful to rewind it so that it began after 'Deck the Halls with Boughs of Holly'. This was Boris's idea of how to keep things going with a swing during the interval.

Jimmy managed to get his order in promptly at the bar, and bought a large whiskey for himself and a large vodka for

Celia to avoid a second scrummage. He was waiting for the right moment to talk to her: later, in bed, he decided, as Susan and Morty Macarthy threw their arms around his neck in greeting.

The performers chatted in an excited group. Boris was suffering badly from nerves and various gins were bought to calm him down. Jimmy and Celia hovered on the edge of things, looking at each other shyly and possessively, each one only waiting for the moment when they could be together in bed and alone with each other.

Ben acted as compère for Boris, who surprised those who had not heard him sing before by the strength and pure pitch of his voice and the liveliness of his act. He sang to the accompaniment of the same tape of great opera hits that Ben and Celia had heard in his car. It turned into another sing-along with the massed humming almost drowning out Boris's well-rehearsed solo.

This, Clarissa told herself, is going to be a hard act to follow. She was tempted to look at just which poems she had randomly plucked from her collection and try, as in other years, to select the lighter, more accessible ones. She could always substitute those for the ones chosen by Lily, and no one would know the difference. But she decided to follow her original plan: she had her preamble, this was her act, and anyway she liked the random element.

She faced a polite silence. One or two people at the back crept out to buy drinks. She began:

'Tonight, instead of reading you work that I think you'll like, I've decided to do some things differently.'

There was some shuffling from the audience as she paused and lifted the leather folder from the chair beside her.

'As some of you may know, this is my third Christmas in Bally C, which means that I have been here for over three years. I had a project when I arrived. I wanted to complete a collection of three hundred poems . . .'

There were a few giggles and some shushing.

'. . . and last week my project was completed.'

The applause was initiated by Ben.

'My poems are filed in tens, and to avoid imposing my own preferences or my ideas of what you might like on you, I have selected at random one group of ten from each hundred. Lily . . .'

Lily sat up straighter at the mention of her name.

'. . . will decide which of the ten in each batch I shall read. Lily, choose a number between one and ten please.'

'Six, my dear.'

Clarissa dramatically turned over five sheets of paper, stopping at the sixth.

Good. A short one in rhyming couplets with some bawdy puns entitled *Mount Cornelia*. Should get a laugh or two, at least from Ben, maybe from Celia and Emily, maybe even from Ian.

It did. Celia, the only one who'd not heard any of Clarissa's verse before, was surprised at her light touch and the absence of her habitual sarcasm. Other members of the audience liked the familiar place names that Clarissa played with, and the applause was more enthusiastic than polite.

Clarissa bowed and smiled and waited for silence.

'Lily. A number between one and ten please.'

'Six, my dear.'

Clarissa did the dramatic turning of the sheets of paper again.

The villanelle.

Oh shit. How dreary. That one *would* have to come up. She'd written it in retrospect about an affair she'd had some years earlier. She began reading reluctantly. It was not partytime stuff:

Life's Bitter Trick

I watch you now with anguish and in pain,

Life's bitter trick, that I should find you here
just when I thought I'd never love again.

I didn't want much more than to stay sane,
an emptiness was all I thought I'd bear;
I watch you now with anguish and in pain

or think about old scars and watch the rain
and hope that maybe hope was in the stare
that you gave me, so full of hurt and strain.

The hope: that one day we can break the chain
that binds you to the children that you share
with a woman who insists you are insane.

Insanity! O madness come again,
that in your darkness I may find a lair
and lick my wounds, unlock my parlous brain,

no more watch *him* with anguish and in pain,
but be myself with exaltation rare
and shout a thousand curses to the air:
Life's bitter trick, that I should find him here.

It was the simple, subdued way that she read it which produced the burst of applause at the end. Lily thought it was a lovely poem, so much nicer than last year's modern ones. Even Celia, still annoyed with Clarissa for her 'Renoiresque' remark, had to concede that this was turning into quite a show. She looked around at Jimmy who'd been separated from her by the Macarthys. He winked.

'Lily?'

'Six, my dear.'

Clarissa paled when she saw the sixth poem of the final batch. But by now the momentum was too great to allow her to cheat. Everyone would notice if she did. She cleared her throat and began a slow chanting reading of a recent work entitled *Roaring Water Bay:*

She stands
in a southerly force seven
on his strand
in the moonlight
waiting for the out-haul
to hear the out-haul
waiting for the out-haul

He said:
To hear the out-haul
in the moonlight
on the strand
in a southerly force seven
would make anyone
write poems
even me.

She
knows he's a poet
because
every time he fucks her
he says
nice?
he asks
nice?
and he fucks her:

nice?
nice?
nice?
And the echoes of his 'nices'
on the strand

in a southerly force seven
in the moonlight
drown the out-haul

O! the out-haul

Celia stumbled to the stairs and made it to the ladies' just in time to throw the contents of her stomach up into the lavatory. Then she retched and sobbed until the sobs turned to deep calming breaths.

She washed her face in cold water and patted it dry with the towel. She seemed to have turned into somebody else: angry, bitter, calm and strong.

There was a knock on the door.

'I say Celia, are you all right?'

Clarissa.

Okay. Get it over with. Now.

Celia opened the door and looked Clarissa in the face, expressionless, she hoped.

'Just tell me one thing. When was the last time you screwed him?'

'Who?'

'For fuck's sake, Jimmy a'course.'

'Jimmy? Whew . . . ages ago, two, three weeks *at least* . . .'

Celia swept past her and down the stairs. The audience were applauding Ian and Ben's guitar recital and rearranging the chairs for the session. Emily and Boris and the Macarthys were handing food around. She failed to locate Jimmy in one quick glance around the room. Perfect. She helped herself to a couple of sandwiches, sorted her coat out from the pile on the floor and put the sandwiches into her pocket. Unnoticed by anyone, she slipped out of Lily's front door.

It took her less than three minutes to change out of her party frock and into her daily uniform of jeans and two sweaters. She picked up her sleeping bag, which she had been using as an extra eiderdown, and her bottles of Christmas Rioja. She was not going to miss the party: she was going to have one on her own. But because Jimmy had a key to her house she was not staying at home.

She ate half a sandwich in the car as the engine warmed up. At the corner of the road she stopped to check the traffic before making a left turn, and in the street light she saw Clarissa come out of Lily's, followed by Jimmy. Celia stared at them. It was like watching actors in a silent film. Clarissa threw her hands up and jabbed a finger at Jimmy. Then one of Jimmy's hands swung down and slapped Clarissa across the face. She lost her balance and fell over sideways, landing heavily on the pavement as Jimmy strode away.

Celia accelerated out of sight before, she hoped, he'd recognised the car. She smiled, and the smile turned into loud laughter which lasted all the way to Emily's. It was far and away the best cabaret act of the evening.

Emily's back door was open as usual. Celia raked up the fire and threw on some more turf, then she put out the lights and settled herself in front of it with a glass of Rioja.

The fire gave her more than warmth. It kept the dark corners away. As she watched the small flames play on the turf she discovered a soothing peace. She could hear Emily's herd shuffling in the byre next door and an occasional lowing. It was good to be alone again with firelight and the mellow wine. Alone again, to carry on. No more illusions, no more hopes of forming half of a perfect couple. Such things simply do not happen. Oneself is all there is. The rest is dreams, transitory illusion. Other people are transitory. You meet, coincide, clash and part. Oneself is all there is. And the fire.

Oneself, thought Celia, looking up at the shadows flickering on the ceiling. What a strange word – oneself, one's self, me. That's all right, me. Alone. I love being alone. The really nice things always happen when I'm on my own. Alone. Because in the end you're always alone. Especially in the end. *Ha*. But in the meanwhile too. Meanwhile we are alone. The rest is . . . *Temporary distraction from the fact of being meanwhile alone. Always.*

She looked beyond the shadows cast by the flames for a pen and paper. This was worth making a note of. It was something oneself often forgot. 'A drop more of this Rioja and I'll be writing bloody poems.' The thought hurt. She hated the idea of poetry. How could anyone do a thing like that? . . . to make her hate poetry . . . forever . . . even Hardy . . . Wind oozing thin through the thorn from nor'ward . . .

Better the fire.

And the beasts.

Their noises comforted her. She closed her eyes and stopped thinking.

'Celia!'

'We saw the car.'

'Where did you get to?'

'Where's Jimmy?'

'Why didn't you stay for the session?'

She had dozed off and it took her a minute to work out that there were only two people addressing her, Emily and Ian. Each, she noticed, carrying a nice, unopened bottle of red wine.

'Hey, you missed all the fun. Someone gave Clarissa a right walloping and she was out cold for about ten minutes. Hit her head on the pavement.'

'We thought you and Jimmy'd left early.'

'Celia, are you all right?'

She smiled sleepily at them. 'Sorry, I must have dozed off. Have a drop of wine?' She groped on the floor for her bottle. At that moment they all heard the clatter of a diesel engine in the boreen.

'Who's that?' Celia asked.

'Dunno. I didn't ask anyone else back.'

'Look, if it's Jimmy I don't want to see him, all right? I'll explain later. Just tell the lousy creep that I've got nothing to say to him.'

'Oh, I see. You two've had a tiff?'

'No. It's all finished. Whatever it was. I just don't want to talk to him.'

The engine stopped and Emily went to the door. The voices reached Celia and Ian as a low drone. Emily came into the room as the engine started up again.

'He says to tell you he'll be back. Most emphatically. That's the only message – "Tell her I'll be back." He was very worried about you, says he's been looking for you all over.'

Celia shrugged. 'Fuck that.'

'So what happened?'

She decided there was no point in telling face-saving lies. Emily and Ian were, at that moment, her closest friends in the world.

'Clarissa's last poem. It was all about Jimmy.'

'The fuck poem?' Emily paused. 'Well, for Christ's sake . . .'

'Bloody 'ell,' said Ian.

'I told you not to mess with that bastard, he's hard as fucking nails, and two-faced with it. And as for Clarissa . . .'

'Look, I'd rather not talk about it, okay? I'm a little confused and maybe I'm a little drunk . . .'

Ian put his arm around her shoulder and said, 'Cheer up luv, it's not the end of the world.'

Celia's eyes filled with tears that kept falling as fast as she brushed them away.

'Hey, we're supposed to be having a party here,' said Emily. 'Ian, put a bloody record on. Loud.'

At six o'clock on Sunday evening Emily phoned Aoife and

Edward as arranged. The children had an extension each and they gabbled away at her.

'Grandma took us shopping.'

'And I saw Father Christmas.'

'And she bought me a party dress *and* a pair of shoes.'

'And he gave me some Lego and Grandma says.'

'And on Monday she's taking me to have my hair cut and *blow dried*.'

'I can have more Lego for Christmas.'

'And Daddy's got a new car.'

'And it's got electric windows.'

'And a super stereo cassette player.'

'And Grandma says that after Christmas we can go shopping for my school uniform.'

'And mine, and football boots, I've got to have football boots.'

'And ballet shoes and a leotard.'

'*What?*'

'Because of our new schools.'

'Grandma says we can go to boarding school and there's an indoor swimming pool at mine.'

'And ballet lessons at mine.'

'Put your father on the line *at once*.'

'Mummy . . .'

'Aoife, go and fetch your father.'

'. . . Mummy, are you cross?'

'No, Edward. I am enraged. Now put down your telephone and let me talk to your father.'

'Mummy, how's Fred?' His cat.

'Freddie's fine. You go back to the television and let me talk to your father, love. I'll phone again on Christmas Day.'

'Bye bye, Mummy.'

'Bye Edward.'

She raged at her ex-husband, then she pleaded, then she tried compromise, Aoife, but not Edward, not for two more years when he'd be eleven. Then she threatened to get the next flight from Cork and fetch them home. Then she wept.

David never could stand scenes so he put his mother on the line. She tried the sweet voice of reason and Emily called her an interfering old bat. Both women hung up at the same moment, each believing she'd cut the other off.

Emily was stunned.

She paced up and down the room alternating between tears of frustration and calm moments when she doubted that the phone call had really happened at all. She felt as if she had been grossly cheated and abused. She knew from the experiences of friends that she could not afford to fight the case legally, and even if she did, and the case was decided in her favour, the courts did not always manage to enforce their decision. It looked as if there was nothing she could do but accept the situation. In one of her fits of weeping she threw herself on her bed fully clothed and fell asleep through sheer emotional exhaustion.

She worked her way through Monday's chores with a fierce energy, one outrageous plan after another churning away in her mind. By five thirty all the essentials had been seen to and she could think of only one thing to do with the rest of the evening: go down to Lily's and, as Ben would put it, get rat-arsed.

Ben and Celia were sitting up at the front bench in silence. The television was on in the back room, and Emily could hear Ian's favourite advertisement which featured a thunderstorm accompanied by a voice of doom that asked: 'Are clouds of doubt hanging over *your* herd? . . . *hoove, roundworm, tapeworm* . . .'

'Hello my dear,' said Lily. 'Not so cold tonight.'

'Isn't it? Gin and tonic please. With ice.'

Ben and Celia turned and looked at Emily. She noticed they were both red-eyed.

'You two been on another spree?' she asked.

They shook their heads and lifted their drinks.

'So what's new?' Emily managed to put a false cheerfulness into her voice.

'Clarissa's disappeared,' said Celia.

'So's Jimmy, and he's taken all the horses with him,' said Ben.

'Except Dún Donncha,' said Celia.

'Whew!' said Emily. 'Talk about soap opera! Who needs bloody *Dallas* when you're living in Bally C? Never a dull moment.'

'You'd better look out,' said Ian, wandering in from the back room. 'Ben might invite you outside and give you a thump on the head.'

'Oh my dears,' said Lily. 'No more knockouts, please. You'll ruin my reputation.'

'That's what I can't understand,' said Celia. 'I *saw* Jimmy hit her, I can't believe they'd run away together after that.'

Ben shrugged. 'Neither can I, but that's what it looks like. Crazy broad. Anyway, who the hell cares?'

'Did anyone see them leave?' asked Emily.

'Yeah. Jimmy went in Con's horse box and Clarissa was driving his jeep.'

'Land Rover,' said Celia. 'And as Ben said, who the hell cares?'

'Shall I change the subject for you?' asked Emily brightly, and she told them her news.

Ben stood up in the shocked silence that followed and lifted Emily off her bar stool in one of his bear hugs.

'Oh, my, Emily,' he shouted. 'This is going to be one hell of a Christmas!'

Clarissa sat in the back of the coach listening to Sibelius on her Walkman (Ben's birthday present last August) and searched for a word to describe her hatred of cities. Cork had been bad enough, but the next stop, via the ferry and another coach, was London. She wondered if she'd survive it.

She looked out into the rainy darkness and caught a glimpse of the floodlit Youghal Carpet Factory and a signpost for Carrigtwohill. She and Ben had gone to a point-to-point there once and Jimmy'd been riding.

Christ, what a crazy bastard. She touched the large bump on the side of her head gently with her fingers. It still ached. An injury which she believed was totally undeserved. Still, Jimmy had at least had the courtesy to call in and apologise the next day, waking her up with the news that Celia and Ben had been spotted having Sunday lunch in the West Cork Hotel. On reflection he decided to believe her story about Ben and Celia, and his disillusionment with Celia was absolute. Just another easy fuck like most of them. He could not understand why he had ever let himself believe anything different.

Clarissa had just enough time to scrounge some empty boxes from Lily and pack her books and notes. She would send for them when she was settled. The rest of her possessions she threw into one big suitcase and she carried the three hundred poems in a large shoulder bag which she gripped tightly on her lap as the bus flashed through the black wet night.

It was over with Ben, and it had nothing to do with Celia. She was welcome to him: a clapped-out, alcoholic old thriller writer. Clarissa had not been able to see it clearly until that blasted poem came up at the cabaret. Life's bitter trick indeed. She knew that Philip Holt was now living somewhere in the West Country. She could find out exactly where when she got to London. Then she was planning to track him down and try again. Maybe his wife had given up on him at last. Maybe this time, with his children three years older, she would get him for good. He was the only man who had ever meant anything to her. Life was a matter of passion and obsession. With Ben there was no passion, that had died long ago, and with the three hundred completed there was no obsession left for her in Bally C. Fuck Bally C and everyone in it, she thought, then she smiled because that was very nearly what she had done . . .

She could imagine them at that very moment, sitting up at the front bench in Lily's – Ben, Celia, Ian, maybe Emily and a few Macarthys – trying to puzzle out the mystery of her disappearance. It would be a typical Bally C evening . . .

A shiver of revulsion went through her at the thought of that familiar dreary scene, the same dreary people, the endless dreary drinks, and she wondered how she'd put up with it so long. But at least she had got what she wanted.

She shifted the weight of the bag on her knees and leant back and closed her eyes with satisfaction. Then she began to work:

The Bally C Collection by Clarissa Lyons?
Bally C by Clarissa Lyons?
South West by Clarissa Lyons?

Christmas Day fell on a Friday that year. Celia, Ben and Ian assembled at Emily's at mid-day and spent the afternoon eating a goose and drinking too much. Small thoughtful presents were exchanged. It wasn't quite as bad as they'd expected: no one broke down, and after the meal Ian helped Emily to milk the herd and then he and Ben got their guitars out and they sang songs together. Emily was advised by her guests to avoid the topic of school when speaking to Aoife and Edward and her phone call was mainly a matter of dutiful appreciation of their Christmas acquisitions. Ben passed out at about nine o'clock and the other three played a reckless game of poker until midnight when Celia lay down in her sleeping bag in front of the fire and Ian and Emily went off to bed.

Since the news of the kidnapping (as they all called the new plans for Aoife and Edward's education) Ian had moved in to Aoife's bedroom, and spent all his time up at Clogheen. Emily liked the company and he was paying for his keep by using his carpentry skills around the house and farm. *Château Despair* was securely tied down by thick ropes and strong tent pegs, its doors and windows tightly fastened against the January gales. The goats were installed up at Cogheen, and on the Monday following Christmas Ian was planning to drive the van up to Cork, deliver it to its new owner and make his way up to the ferry at Rosslare.

Emily had tried to convince him to stay, and so had Celia. Ben had offered to lend him the money he needed to keep the van on the road, but Ian was stubbornly independent and refused to get into debt.

He had also discovered that after living in a caravan for three years – one in Galway and two in Bally C – certain material ambitions were asserting themselves very strongly.

He worried about whether his current materialism was a sign of age – he was just twenty-eight – and whether he was finally losing the ideals that he had always tried to live up to: ideals of simplicity and non-acquisivitiveness. His material ambitions were, he consoled himself, still fairly simple, almost minimal. He would like to live in a house, not a caravan, and have a decent piece of land to call his own, not an illegally fenced-in postage stamp. He wanted to grow vegetables, establish fruit bushes and an asparagus bed. He wanted to increase his herd of goats. He wanted an out-house in which to store wood, and another in which to work on it. For the summer he would like to own a small fishing boat, maybe sixteen foot, with an outboard engine. He also wanted some new cassette tapes, a new cassette player, a Walkman, and he desperately wanted a proper stereo. In really dark moments he would admit to himself that he would also very much like to own a colour television set and video recorder. All this was in addition to keeping the van on the road and buying a couple of pairs of jeans and one of those heavy-duty parkas like the ones that Ben and Clarissa had.

It was not a very long list, nor a particularly unrealistic one. Many of his friends had all those things and more, but then they also had regular jobs, i.e. they had sold their souls to the system. Ian knew that was what you had to do when *things* started to matter more than *living*. What disturbed him was that he had started to suspect that things made living more worthwhile. Once you had things (even such basic things as a van on the road) you started to live better. But you could only get the things by temporarily abandoning the living side of it. He knew himself well enough to be reasonably sure that a few months' hard work would convince him again that it was better to be living without things than to sell your soul, and he'd be back. But first he had to go, in order to purge the bitterness which was accumulating in him because of his lack of things.

He tried to explain this to Celia and Emily. It seemed that Celia sort of understood, but Emily said that if he knew he was going to come running back as soon as he got fed up with working, then why bother to go in the first place, which made him think that she didn't understand at all. That was a shame, because he liked Emily a lot now that he had stopped being in awe of her. Since the kidnapping she was no longer the General, but seemed to be just as confused and mixed up as Ian.

Celia went back to her house on St Stephen's Day, and stayed indoors for three days, sunk in a deep lethargy. Ben called to invite her for a drink in Lily's and she declined, saying that she needed to be alone for a while. He nodded and left in silence.

She watched one movie after another on her cranky old black and white television. She left it on from morning to closedown, whether she was watching anything or not.

By Monday evening she knew most of the advertisements off by heart.

It snowed a little on Monday afternoon, an unusual occurrence in West Cork. She watched the children outside her window in the dusk scraping up the pathetic sprinkling of flakes, making them into snowballs, and screaming at the cold wetness as they pelted each other. She drew the curtains and turned back to the television.

She felt as if she had put on at least a stone in weight since the cabaret. Her waist had thickened, and those awful pockets were forming on her hips again. She was as angry with Jimmy for having taken the horses away with no word of warning as she was about his two-timing her with Clarissa. The routine of riding out every morning had been shaping her days, and she had grown used to the constant challenge of dealing with the beautiful high-spirited animals.

She decided that when Jimmy turned up again (he had said he'd be back, that was the only message he had left for her) she would overcome her disgust at his running off with Clarissa, and offer to ride out his horses on the original friendly basis. There was no doubt in her mind that Jimmy and Clarissa were together, up in Mallow at the stud farm, and, what was worse, they were with the horses and she was not. Clarissa couldn't stand animals. It was totally unfair.

On the evening of the Tuesday Celia decided to go down to Lily's in the hope that Con would be there and would have some news of Jimmy, and, more importantly, the horses. Bally C Lady was being schooled up at the stud farm along with Jimmy's horses. Perhaps now she could talk to Con more calmly than on their last nightmarish meeting when he'd called at her house on the night after the cabaret to let her know that the horses had gone and she would not be needed at the yard the following morning. She had been so dumbstruck that she had not even asked him in.

Lily's was hushed. Everyone looked utterly miserable –

Lily, Emily, Ben, Boris, even Con and Barney Mack. Lily, Emily and Ben were crying. Celia stopped in her tracks as two gardai walked past her and out of the door bidding her goodnight in low voices. Then a wail started up:

'Celia, he's dead.'

'Yesterday evening.'

'Came off the road at Leap.'

'Died on the way to the Regional.'

'The creature.'

'God rest his soul.'

'FOR CHRIST'S SAKE, WHO?'

'Ian.'

'Ian.'

'Ian.'

'Ian.'

'Ian.'

'Ian.'

JANUARY

Lily and Emily took charge of the funeral arrangements on behalf of Ian's brother. He'd been contacted by the police in London, and flew in with his wife on New Year's Eve. Celia and Ben drove up to meet them at the airport.

Ian's brother Tony was a quiet, conservative man, a devout Catholic and a very moderate drinker. He was some years older than Ian. Ian had lived with Tony and his wife Jean after the death of his parents when he was fourteen years old, so they felt his death as the loss of a son.

Everyone agreed that Ian would want to be buried in Bally C. The funeral arrangements were announced in the deaths column of the *Cork Examiner*, the same paper that had carried a full report of the fatal accident.

The body arrived from Cork at six o'clock on the evening before the funeral. A big crowd attended the simple removal service. The church was full.

The coffin was placed in front of the altar and a decade of the rosary was said over it. Tony and Jean and half a dozen of Ian's closest friends sat in a place of honour in the front pews and at the end of the service the entire congregation waited while they left the church.

There were drinks afterwards at Cogheen. Emily and Celia had baked a leg of ham and made a huge bowl of potato salad and another of coleslaw. Ben carried a tray around and offered the company a choice of red whiskey or white whiskey. Lily's was closed for the evening out of respect.

Many friends of Ian had travelled some distance to attend both the removal and the Requiem Mass which was to be said the following morning. Emily was billeting them on to neighbours with spare rooms. Celia got a bearded musician from Galway, his girlfriend, and Ian's friend from Cork city who'd wanted to buy the van.

It was, at first, an awkward event. There were about twenty strangers who knew nobody. The local crowd were inhibited by Tony and Jean's presence. The more sensitive among them feared that Tony might be upset by the prodigious consumption of alcohol and subsequent boisterous behaviour which was customary on such an occasion.

People were standing in small groups holding stilted conversations, when Jimmy walked in carrying a six-pack of beer. Emily gave him a glass of whiskey and they exchanged a few words. Then she took him over to Tony and Jean and he shook their hands and spoke to them for a few minutes. While he was with them, Emily shot over to Ben and whispered something in his ear. His face lit up and he started laughing. Everyone turned to watch. He put down his tray and went through the door to the scullery leaving a puzzled silence behind him.

'Celia! Celia!' She was standing at the table pouring tea into cups on a tray. She looked at Ben's beaming face and listened to his manic laughter and for a second she believed that he had finally cracked up. He grabbed her shoulders.

'Clarissa's in London!'

'What?'

'She never ran off with Jimmy. She drove his jeep up to Cork and took the coach to Rosslare.'

The cloud of gloom in which Celia had been living for the past two weeks lifted. She felt a strange sensation in her lips – a smile, which was followed by a laugh.

'Is Jimmy here?'

'Yeah. He just arrived.'

'Oh, Ben!' She was going to tell him that she'd didn't know what to do when a sound from next door silenced her. Jimmy was playing a sad air on the tin whistle. She and Ben crept back in to the room and stood in silence with everyone else, looking at the floor. There was a cheer and a burst of applause when he finished. Then the musician from Galway produced his fiddle and Con fetched his gadget from Barney Mack's car. Someone assembled a flute and a bodhran appeared. Daniel sent Ownie to fetch his twelve string, Celia picked up a couple of spoons from the table and Ben went into Aoife's bedroom and came back with Ian's guitar.

The session lasted until four in the morning. Celia was watching for an opportunity to be alone with Jimmy, but it never came. He appeared to be deliberately avoiding her. This confirmed her fear that Clarissa had told him about her 'affair' with Ben. Everything was bloody awful, and she had no idea how to get herself out of the mess. She stared at the floor as Barney Mack's cracked and tuneless voice began yet another of his interminable rebel songs:

'Come gather round me boyos
And listen to my song . . .

An arm was round her shoulder and a voice sang close to her ear in a whisper:

'It is extr-e-e-e-mely boring
and it is extr-e-e-e-mely long.'

Ben, with one of Ian's old jokes.

'You'll feel better after the funeral,' he said, and he squeezed her hand.

Celia looked up at Ben with tears in her eyes, and as she did so she saw Jimmy stare at the two of them, then turn away with a look of contempt on his face and leave the room.

Emily got barely three hours' sleep that night. She was up before first light to feed and milk her dairy herd, feed and milk Ian's goats and collect eggs. The latter had been

Aoife's chore. She was starting to miss the children's help around the place as well as their company.

Ben and some strangers had done most of the clearing up the night before, but had left all the washed and dried delft on the table. Emily stoked up the range and fetched in more fuel, then she started to put away the dishes. By the time that Tony and Jean came downstairs the place had been restored to its normal state and rashers were frying in a big pan.

It was a wild day with a strong westerly wind carrying sheets of rain in from the Atlantic.

Celia was standing in the porch of the church shaking the rain off her oilskins when Emily arrived with Tony and Jean. They went ahead while Emily waited for Celia.

'I'm dreading this bloody Mass,' said Emily. 'I wouldn't have come if it hadn't been for those two. Ian never went near the damn church.'

'I quite like a good funeral,' said Celia. 'I just wish it wasn't Ian's.'

'The creature,' said Emily, imitating Lily's lament, for want of a better way to express her feelings. Celia was not amused.

It was a weekday morning, but even so the church was almost as full as it had been on the previous night. Celia was not the only person in Bally C with a fondness for funerals. The choir and the organ master were present, and Emily and Celia sat near the alcove. They noticed that some of the strangers, Ian's old friends from Galway who'd been at the session the night before, were sitting with the choir. Lily and Jean had organised the religious side of Ian's funeral so neither Emily nor Celia knew what to expect this morning.

Slow tuneless organ music announced the entrance of the priest. Celia wondered if she was going to cry again. Her reaction to Ian's death was still mixed with the relief she'd felt that night in Lily's on hearing that the name of the dead man was Ian, and not Jimmy as she'd feared for a few terrible seconds. She stared at the solid polished coffin and forced herself to think exclusively about Ian for the rest of the Mass.

It was the first time since the news of Ian's death that Emily had been alone with her thoughts and not distracted by chores and practicalities. As she stood and knelt and sat with the rest of the congregation she began to face up to the fact of the kidnapping, and turn possible plans over in her mind. She noticed the Macarthys arriving during the Gospel and slipping into a pew on the opposite side of the church. She smiled at the sight of Morty and Daniel in well-pressed suits. Daniel had a strong conservative streak which was seldom evident. Charlie was not with them, but she tracked him down, standing at the back of the church with Con and Barney Mack wearing his usual old bomber jacket and jeans.

She found that she had sat through the priest's eulogy, whose platitudes she had been dreading, without hearing a word. Perhaps there had not been one at all. She stood for the Creed feeling relatively cheerful. It was all downhill from here. Once the Creed was sung the worst of the Mass was over as far as Emily was concerned.

She wished that Celia would not be so hearty in her participation. Apart from being irritated by this evidence of an unsuspected religiosity in her friend, Celia's voice was horribly out of tune and destroyed the enjoyment Emily might otherwise have had from the harmonies of the choir.

Celia in turn was annoyed by Emily's fidgeting. If she wanted to be looking around her all the time why didn't she stand at the back with the men? And there was no point in checking her wristwatch every few seconds. The Mass would take as long as a Mass always took and a bit more for the final blessing of the coffin.

In no time at all, it seemed to Celia, that terrible final moment had come. The priest walked slowly down the altar steps towards the coffin with the aspergillum raised in his right hand. A small altar-boy followed him carrying the holy water. She did not notice that two men in the front row of the choir had stood up, one with a fiddle and the other with a flute, until the flute player startled her by blowing a long shaky note, and then another. Then the fiddle player came in on a higher note, also a little uncertain. The hairs on the back of Celia's head stood up, prickling. The fiddle player's foot was tapping away, the flute found the melody, the fiddle found the rhythm and they were together, the sharpness of the fiddle contrasting with the flute's mellowness and producing a beautiful air, at once sprightly and stately. This was the right way to bury Ian, Celia thought, the right way to bury everyone when their time came: with peace and dignity and ceremony.

The music ended and was followed by a tense silence, as if everyone in the church were holding their breath. Then a great sigh seemed to sweep through the crowd as the priest gave the blessing and the pall bearers moved towards the coffin.

It was less than a mile to the graveyard, and some people chose to walk in spite of the squalls of rain still blowing in from the west. The group of foot-mourners straggled behind the hearse, leading a tail of familiar local cars.

Soon they had left the last buildings of Bally C behind them and were on the high-hedged coastal road. Through gaps in the bare blackthorn there were glimpses of the open sea, grey and troubled.

Celia stayed at some distance from the graveside crowd and wandered among other overgrown plots as the mourners gathered closer to the priest who was starting a final decade of the rosary. It was almost too much. Poor Ian, one moment of misjudgement on an icy curve and finish. The End. It could have been any one of them. Why him?

Her gloomy thoughts were interrupted by the sound of scuffling from behind a nearby headstone, a large well-weathered Celtic cross. She heard angry whispering:

'Willya let me alone ya fucker?'

'Shut yer fuckin' mouth and get over there and say the fuckin' rosary.'

'I will not.'

Crack.

Daniel walked away from the headstone towards Ian's grave with a snarl on his face. He did not seem to notice Celia standing in his path and she leapt aside just in time to avoid him. Then she picked her way across the rough grass to the stone he had left, wondering what she would find.

It was Charlie, slumped against the grey cross spitting blood out of his mouth and wiping it away with the back of his hand.

Celia squatted beside him.

'Charlie! Are you all right?'

He shook his head and stuck his tongue out. 'I think he got my other front tooth,' he said in a slurred voice. 'Disgraceful thing to do at a funeral. My own brother.'

Celia agreed. 'Let's get you out of here before they finish,' she said, putting an arm under his elbow. 'That way no one will notice.'

She walked Charlie back to her house where he rinsed out his mouth and inspected the damage. The tooth was still there, it was only the gum that had been cut. He seemed to think he'd got off lightly.

'So much for the season of peace on earth and goodwill to all men,' he said. 'First Clarissa, now me. I'll be glad when it's over!' And he laughed a little unsteadily.

'What was it all about?'

'Yerra bossy-boots elder brother, fuckin' goodie-two-shoes.' He sounded so much like a nine-year-old that Celia nearly laughed herself.

'Do you think Ian gives a fuck whether I wear my feckin' suit to his funeral or not? I will not have Daniel thinking he can go telling me what to do.'

'It does seem a bit much.'

'He's a hard man,' said Charlie. 'But this time I'm going to make him pay for it. I'm going to feck off and he and his fecking string band can go stew.' He laughed more loudly.

Celia knew that Daniel was about to start auditioning musicians for the band and rehearsing for its professional debut. He and Charlie talked of little else.

'But there'd be no band without you.'

'Exactly. I'll take the first job going, even if it's in Rangoon. All the better if it is!' His laugh was almost demonic by now. 'Come on down to Lily's for a celebration.'

'But what about Daniel? Won't he be down in Lily's too?'

'He will, but he'll go north and I'll go south and it won't be the first time either.'

The atmosphere in Lily's that lunchtime was festive. Everyone seemed to be under compulsion to let off steam after the solemn funeral. The conversation was loud and jocular and covered every imaginable topic except Ian. Charlie stayed near the front door while Daniel stood near the door to the backroom. They ignored each other, and as far as Celia could tell, nobody seemed to notice Charlie's fat lip.

She stood a little apart from the rest, pretending to listen to Boris recounting details of the Christmas which he had spent with some Dutch friends in Kerry. She had been counting on Ben being in Lily's, and was planning to persuade him to explain things to Jimmy. But he hadn't turned up.

She could not stop herself watching Jimmy who was up at his usual end of the bar with Con and Barney Mack. She was aware that he too was watching her, and once Con caught her eye and winked, which made her suspect that they were talking about her.

Jimmy was staring at her now, staring so intently that she

felt he was looking right through her. She looked back at him with a desperate pleading in her eyes, willing him to cross the room and talk to her, to give her a chance to explain.

He didn't move. Then he looked away and leant across to listen to Barney Mack's mumblings, a slight smile on his face.

Celia could stand it no longer. She drained her hot whiskey and made her way across the room, clumsily pushing chatting groups apart with loud 'sorrys' and 'excuse mes' in order to place her empty glass on the bar next to Jimmy.

'Could you drop by a bit later?' she said. 'There's something I'd like to explain.'

'Oh aye . . .' She was not sure if his answer was interrogative or affirmative, but it was certainly cold.

Celia waited for Jimmy in her front room all afternoon and all evening. She did nothing except to stoke the wood burner and sit in an armchair watching it.

Once she heard a diesel engine stop outside her window and she ran to the front door but it was not Jimmy.

Time and again she thought of putting on her coat and going out to look for him, but every time she fought off the impulse. It would look desperate. To look desperate would make her look guilty, and if she looked guilty it would be that much more difficult to convince Jimmy that her story was true. In any case, it was not up to her to make all the effort: Jimmy also had some explaining to do.

She considered going to look for Ben, and trying to persuade him to do the explaining. But that seemed cowardly. Ben would probably not want to have anything to do with Jimmy, and anyway Celia suspected (quite rightly) that Ben was probably blind drunk by now.

It was one in the morning before she could allow herself to admit that Jimmy was not coming to look for her.

The next day Jimmy went back to Mallow. Celia saw him leave Bally C as she was walking home from the supermarket. She waved at the Land Rover and he accelerated up the Cork road without acknowledging her. His apparent indifference froze something inside her. She did not understand how a man who had only recently been so close as both friend and lover could cut her off without even giving her the chance to explain.

Her anger was fed by the righteousness of the innocent. If Jimmy was prepared to believe the first rumour he heard about her without asking for confirmation then he was a shallow suspicious fool as well as a heartless two-timing bastard.

But her anger was not enough to prevent her falling into a state of indolence and depression. Only two weeks ago she had been fully occupied all day. Now she had nothing to do: no horses, no pasties, no rehearsals, no man. The weather was persistently cold and rainy and she had a heavy head cold which stopped her going for walks. Instead she got up at midday and sat in front of the fire reading the tatty paperbacks which circulated among the regulars in Lily's. Around four o'clock when the sun started to set she pulled the curtains. At six o'clock she turned on the television news and then watched whatever was going for the rest of the evening.

She did not like to admit it in the daytime, but sometimes, as she lay awake at night, she would face the fact that without Jimmy and the horses there no longer seemed much reason for staying in Bally C.

But neither did there seem to be any reason to move elsewhere. She hated the idea. Not until the money threatened to run out, and even then she'd be reluctant.

Nothing could be settled until Jimmy came back.

Meanwhile it was a question of hanging on. Despite everything.

Celia's absence from Lily's was causing some concern. She had not been seen out walking, and neither had she been shopping in Bally C for at least two days. Ben volunteered to go up and check that she was all right.

He found her watching the six o'clock news with both hands clasped around a mug of tea.

'You look like death,' he said.

'Thanks. That makes me feel just great.'

'They're all asking for you, so I came up to see how you are.'

'Just a filthy cold. Have a seat.'

'Thanks.' He produced a noggin of whiskey. 'Put a drop of that in your tea.' She obeyed.

'So how's things?' he said.

She looked at him with watery eyes.

'Still no word from the half-sir?'

She shook her head. Ben took her hand. 'That'll blow over, you wait and see. These things happen all the time. Look, if it's any help, I'll explain it all to Jimmy. The minute he walks into Lily's.'

'Would you really?'

'Sure thing.'

'Thanks.' She sighed. 'Any news of Clarissa?'

'Not a word. She'll write me soon. She has to, I've got her books. But the mail's all fucked after the holidays so I guess I'll just have to wait. Crazy broad won't use a phone, can you get *that?*'

'She lives in the right place then.' The inefficiency of Bally C's telephone system was legendary.

'Not any more she doesn't.'

'You don't think she's coming back?'

'Hell, no. And if she does I will personally kick her arse all the way from here to Skibbereen.'

Ben seemed to be restored to his usual loud-mouthed self, and Celia envied the clear-cut end to his affair with Clarissa. She'd often been through the same thing. A clean break was always easier to handle than a small hope. That way, even Nick's defection had not hurt much.

She remembered that August day when she first came across Ben and Clarissa, and how perfect the prospect of living in Bally C had been, and she wondered at her ability to turn such a quiet, beautiful place into something which was now nothing more than a vast dark corner with the light impossibly remote.

It was not really Edward's puzzled and tearful phone call from his new school that made Emily decide to sell up, but it gave her sufficient impetus to drive straight to Skibbereen where she found herself sitting in the estate agent's office.

Life at Clogheen was too bleak without the children. They had given a focus to her days which she had now lost entirely. She was doing no work at all in her glasshouses, and spending far too many aimless hours in Lily's.

Her first plan had been to stay on in the hope that she could win the children back, but this was looking ever more unlikely. So far Aoife was enjoying her new school, and David had written a very pleasant letter to report on the progress of his relationship with Edward. It would be unfair to deprive the child of his father.

She was still seething with resentment at not having been consulted on the original plans. However, the original plans did not include the possibility of Emily selling up and moving to a place near Edward's school. There could be no objection then to Edward living with her and attending the school as a day-boy. That would be a victory of a sort, and it would reunite her with Edward. But with the current state of the property market it was a challenge, even to someone of such renowned competence as the General, to manage such a move.

The man who had sold her Clogheen twelve years before had handed the business over to his nephew, a bright young fellow who'd spent most of his working life in the States. He knew Clogheen, and his plan for disposing of it seemed brilliantly simple to Emily, though it was not without an element of risk. He advised her to sell the land and the house separately. There was nothing in the deeds to prevent her. He knew of one farmer (Emily could guess which one) who would almost certainly make her a good offer for the land and the glasshouses. Then they would put the house and half an acre of garden on the market as a separate lot. If it didn't move with local advertising he had connections in London, Amsterdam and Hamburg who would advertise it as a holiday home. He warned her that it could take a year or more to sell, but he believed that if she held out for her price she would get it eventually.

She said she would think it over, and drove home in a much more cheerful mood.

Lily often promised herself that she would shut up shop for January and February, but when it came to it she never did, though she certainly made no profit in those months. Her shop stocked only packaged and tinned foods, and was the last resort for groceries. She had few visitors in the day. In the evenings she sat behind the bar looking after the two or three customers who wandered in for a pint.

Tuesday, dole day, was the only busy time of the week. By Wednesday the dole cheques had been spent and only Ben was left in the bar, with occasional visits from Con and Barney Mack and Emily and Boris.

So far this Wednesday night was turning out to be one that, for the time of year, Lily could almost call busy. Ben and Boris and Emily were playing cards by the fire in the back room. Con and Barney Mack were up at the bar. Then the door swung open and in walked Celia.

'Lily.'

'Hallo my dear. Are you over your cold now? I was sorry to hear you were sick.'

'I am surviving,' said Celia as Con slid his arm around her waist and gave her a playful tickle.

'Con! Stop it!'

'Yerragoaway, gerral! I'll take that puss off yer! Lily! Fillum up here.'

'Ye're full up yourself Con Leary.' Lily looked enquiringly at Celia. 'A hot one?'

'Please.'

'Never mind them, gerral. They've been all day long at the mart.' Lily's accent, like Jimmy's, always slipped into broadest West Cork when talking to Con and Barney Mack. Celia felt at home in this company. It reminded her of the horses.

'Were you buying or selling?' she asked Con.

'*He* thinks he's after buying a fine herda pure breds,' said Con, pointing at Barney Mack. 'I tell 'oo,' and he laughed quietly. Barney Mack finished coughing then shouted at the floor, 'He knows as much about pure breds as I know about wheelbarrers.' Barney Mack's ferocity made Celia jump. 'And I know feck all about wheelbarrers. Feck all!'

'I tell 'oo,' said Con again, putting his arm around Celia's waist. Then he whispered in her ear, 'Will 'oo be lonesome tonight? Will 'oo come up for a bit of a court?' His china blue eyes were more full of fun than lust. 'Will 'oo give me a spin?'

'None a' that talk Con Leary.' Lily had sharp hearing.

This time it was Barney Mack who laughed: 'I tell 'oo, she's a big machine and she have her own wedding tackle. She have no use for 'oo boy! She's a big machine.'

Celia did not like being spoken of as a big machine. While Con could get away with murder because of his twinkling eyes, Barney Mack's remarks always seemed to fall with a leaden thump far beyond the boundaries of her sense of humour. She moved up the bar leaving two empty seats between herself and Con. The men calmed down.

Con pushed his pint nearer to his drop and took a sip from the latter. 'Never 'oo mind gerral,' he said. 'We'll give 'oo a spin next week to take the puss off-a-ya.'

Celia did not understand.

'Ye'll have the wedding tackle back in town and he'll give 'oo a good ride.'

Barney Mack's remark had not made it any clearer to her, but he and Con were rocking with laughter.

'If he don't, he's a bollax of a man.'

'A right bollax.'

'Gerrawayoutathat talk the pair of yeeze,' said Lily, moving to the other end of the bar opposite Celia.

'We'll have 'oo up on the Lady next week and we'll see did she get any learning above in Malla.'

At last Con was making sense. Celia did indeed lose her sour-puss. 'When will they be back?'

'Sunday evening. We'll ride out the three of us Monday morning. Half-eight sharp.'

'Lily, a pint please and . . .' She gestured toward the men.

It was wonderful. Whatever happened with Jimmy, and now that he and horses were coming back, *something* must happen, she would at least be working Bally C Lady again for Con. Con wanted her to ride out for him, so whether or not she patched things up with Jimmy, she was back in the saddle.

'We've only a week then to Killer,' said Con, suddenly sober and businesslike.

'Killer?' said Celia.

'Killeagh' said Lily. 'The first point-to-point of the season. It's a grand day out.'

'Are you going?' Celia did not know that Lily followed the horses.

Lily stopped knitting and leant forward: 'If I get a spin I like the day out and I get Pake in to do the bar. And later in the season, the Carbery meeting is grand, you'd find people at the Carbery point-to-point that you knew long 'go and haven't seen to talk to for years and years.'

'Hi there, stranger.' Ben was obviously in a good mood. 'Lily, same again please.' He turned to Celia. 'Can I interest you in a game of poker? Ten pence in and half the pot maximum bet?'

Celia knew she shouldn't be gambling with her limited resources, but the temptation of a few hours' play in congenial company was too great to resist. She had to do something to celebrate the news about the horses, and poker was marginally better than simply getting langers.

'Okay.' She picked up her drink and her purse.

'You don't have to wait to be asked, you know.'

'I wasn't waiting to be asked. I was talking to Con.'

She went into the back room and pulled a chair up to the table where Emily and Boris were waiting.

'Hallo Celia.'

'Emily. How's things?'

'Grand. I'm just back from the mart. Got rid of the goats.'

'Any news from Aoife and Edward?'

'Term started last week for both of them.'

'Poor little buggers,' said Ben, taking his seat at the table again. 'Whose deal?'

'Mine,' said Boris. 'And Celia and Emily are shy.'

Each woman pushed a coin in the middle of the table and the game got under way.

'Four threes,' said Celia.

'House. Aces high,' said Ben.

'Thank God I dropped out of that one,' said Emily.

'So I pay the presents and I quit the game,' said Boris. 'You have cleaned me out.'

Celia scooped the pile of coins and notes towards her corner of the table and took an extra pound from each player as a present for her hand of four of a kind. She reckoned she had quadrupled her money in two hours' play. It was unprecedented. When she needed to win, she usually lost.

'Same again?' she asked, offering the ritual present-winner's round in accordance with the house rules.

Boris declined, and went off for an early night. When Celia got back to the table Emily was reading a big sheet of white paper covered in Clarissa's large handwriting.

'Did you hear about the mail man?' asked Ben, pointing at a chair piled with muddy letters and periodicals.

'No. What about him?'

'He's been off on a spree since New Year's Eve. Dumps the goddamn mail in a ditch every morning and goes up to the Hilton to get rat-arsed. Barney Mack just happened to see him dumping it this morning, and rescued what he could. Out of the ditch. Including a letter from Clarissa.'

'Was there anything for me?' She had a very faint hope that Jimmy might have sent some sort of message.

'No. Barney Mack woulda given it to you.'

'What's Clarissa got to say?'

Emily looked up from the letter. 'She's renting a place in the West Country quite near Edward's school. I'm going to ask her to visit him, maybe she can take him out for a Sunday. He says he hates Sunday there.'

'Looks like she got what she wanted,' said Ben. 'A book of poems coming out in September, and a biography of Lockhart commissioned.'

'Who's Lockhart?'

'A poet. Snuffed it in the late 'fifties. Clarissa always thought he was under-rated and it looks like she's convinced someone else.'

'So she's not coming back.' Celia wanted Ben to confirm it.

Ben laughed. 'If that crazy goddamn bitch ever sets foot in Bally C again I'm getting up a lynch party.'

'Count me in,' said Celia.

Emily was copying Clarissa's address on to a beer mat and not listening. 'I think I'll drop in on her when I go to England,' she said. 'That way I could take her books over. She seems to be worried about them.'

'She's afraid I might go have a bonfire,' said Ben. 'It's one hell of a tempting idea.'

'I didn't know you were going to England,' said Celia. It was remarkable how much news one missed by not going down to Lily's.

'I'm going for half-term,' said Emily. 'I'm thinking of selling up and I want to have a look at what's available over there.'

'I thought you said a two-bedroom flat,' said Celia.

'That was if I went to London. The idea now is to get somewhere near Edward's school so that he can be a day-boy. It'll be much smaller than Clogheen, no room for a herd, but I wouldn't mind concentrating on veg. You don't have to milk them, for a start.'

Celia was not sure whether she'd be sorry to see Emily go or not. She caught Con Leary winking at her from the bar, and she smiled back at him.

Probably not.

Celia was curled up in one of her fireside chairs absorbed in the final pages of an early Dick Francis thriller when there was a knock at the door.

It was Charlie carrying two large guitar cases and ruck-sack, with his blond hair hanging in dark wet rat's tails. For a second she thought it was Ian.

'Charlie! Come in, you're soaking.'

'Thanks.' He dumped his stuff in her hallway and went over to the woodburner where his clothes and hair began to steam.

'You're grand and snug in here,' he said. 'That's the way to be on a day like this.'

'Would you like a cup of tea?'

'I'd nearly kill for one!' said Charlie, and laughed his raucous laugh.

When Celia had the two mugs poured she said, 'So where are you off to?'

'München.'

'What?'

'München. Munich. Krautland. The place where Boris does not come from. I've come down to say goodbye.'

'Well!'

'I've a job in a band,' he sounded very pleased with himself. 'Yer aul plinkety-plonk stuff and the rousing rebel songs but what the fuck? Good crack for a few months.'

'Is Daniel going too?'

'The brother and I are still incommunicado. And he'll be out for my blood again when he finds I've fecked off with the twelve-string. He'll be raging!' Charlie laughed even louder than before.

Celia thought that was a rotten thing to do to Daniel, but she did not want to get involved in a family feud so she kept the conversation on neutral ground until there was another knock on the door.

'That'll be my spin to Cork,' said Charlie, and gave Celia a damp farewell kiss.

It seemed that January was provoking a mass exodus from Bally C and Celia was wondering who else was likely to join it when there was yet another knock on the front door.

It was Daniel this time, looking even more dishevelled than usual.

'Have you seen that brother of mine?'

'Charlie? He left a few minutes ago. Didn't you see him on the road?'

'Shit. He musta been in that van.'

'Whose?'

'Some stranger.'

'Someone called for him, I'm not sure who. Come in a minute, you're freezing the house out.'

Daniel paced up and down Celia's tiny sitting room like a clockwork toy.

'For god's sake Daniel, sit down and have a cup of tea.'

'He's fucked up everything. I'll never get Susan to stay now, and without Susan and Charlie I'll never get the class of musician I wanted . . . there's no point to the whole thing now that he's gone. The Macarthy String Band with only one Macarthy. Shit.'

'Well, I think it was rotten of him to take the twelve-string as well . . .'

'*What?*'

'Your twelve-string . . . didn't you know?' She was thinking she'd really let herself in for it now, and was expecting to become the victim of one of Daniel's notorious fits of anger but instead of raging he simply sat down in an armchair.

'I'm really sorry Daniel,' said Celia. 'Couldn't you borrow one from someone?'

'Yerra fuck it. I'll do something else.'

'What?'

'I'll think it over. Every time we try to get the show on the road someone fucks up. And every time it happens I find that I don't fucking care.'

'Why not?'

'I've plenty of other talents,' he said, giving Celia a crooked smile. She liked his self-confidence. It seemed to be more than idle boasting. 'This way I can keep the music for pure enjoyment. You won't catch me selling out to the Swedish plinkety-plonk market.'

'He's gone to Munich.'

'Maybe. He told Lily it was Sweden. So as to confuse me, you understand. Charlie is not a liar.'

Celia liked Daniel for making this defence of Charlie. Her opinion of 'bossy-boots elder brother' was improving by the minute. He obviously took the responsibilities of that position very seriously, and it seemed that his fierce temper was not indiscriminate, but mainly directed towards keeping the family in order. He now struck Celia as being a far more mature and interesting person than Charlie. She understood something of why Daniel often looked harassed and was less fun to be with than Charlie, and she was sorry that it had taken her so long to get to know him.

There was a poker game going on in the back room on Saturday night when Jimmy reappeared in Lily's. Celia was facing the door, and was the first to see him. She was not sure whether the sudden emotion that struck her was love or hate.

'Celia! Are you opening?'

She looked automatically at her cards, then put them face down on the table.

'No. I'm not playing.'

'But you've just . . . ah, crazy broad.' Ben turned to the next player. Celia waited until the hand was won, then leant over to Ben.

'Jimmy's just come in,' she said.

'What about it?'

'Ben, you promised, the minute he walked in the door you said.'

'Now?'

'Yes. Now.'

'Okay, okay. Deal me out for this hand.'

'And me,' said Celia.

'What's going on?' asked Emily.

'Two minutes,' said Ben.

Celia went upstairs to the ladies. It was the best way she could think of to kill time. When she came back Ben was sitting at the table again.

'All clear,' he said as she approached. She walked on past him and up to the bar where Jimmy was, as usual, talking to Con and Barney Mack. She stood beside Jimmy and waited for a break in the discussion.

'Jimmy?'

'Hallo Celia.' Neutral and polite.

'Would you mind coming over to the house for a minute?'

He stood up and apologised to Con and walked over to the shop counter opposite the bar. Celia followed.

'I think whatever has to be said can be said here.'

Celia stared at him. Not here, in public, no, it couldn't. But she said nothing. Jimmy went on in a low calm voice.

'It didn't work and we both got hurt. I don't care what was or was not going on, we made a mess of it and there's an end to it. I've no time for messing.'

He paused as if expecting Celia to say something, and when she kept silent he spoke again, this time in a businesslike voice: 'If you want to ride out with me next week I'd appreciate it. If you don't, then I understand perfectly.'

'But I do, a'course.'

He smiled at her sudden animation, then went on: 'You remember what I said at the beginning? That I'd rather have the friendship than the other complications?'

'Yes.'

'So we'll be friends.'

'We will a'course.'

Celia blew her nose and said, 'Excuse me, I've a terrible cold.' Then she walked into the back room and picked up her coat, mentioning her cold again to the poker players as a pretext for wanting an early night.

She sat up in bed with the light on for a long time trying to sort out her feelings about Jimmy. She had expected an apology and another chance. But Jimmy had shown himself to be so cold and had given up so easily that maybe she was better off with only his friendship and his horses and without that which he referred to as 'the other complications'.

Complications brought nothing but misery. She listened to the wind whining around the telegraph wires across the road and thought that she could faintly hear the out-haul. A southerly. Force seven at least. It still hurt. There would definitely be no other complications. Just friendship.

FEBRUARY

'Hallo there.'

'Hallo.'

She walked into the yard trying to behave as if it were just any old Monday morning, any old morning in November when it had all been beginning, and not their first ride together since the morning of the cabaret.

Jimmy was threading a martingale onto a bridle and behaving as usual, keeping up a pleasant flow of conversation while absorbed in his task:

'That's a fine pair of breeches.'

'They're some old ones I had in storage. My father posted them to me. They still fit, just.' (But only because she had let a piece of material into the back seam to allow her to do up the zip.)

Jimmy looked at her hard. 'What weight are you now?'

'Ten and a half.' There was no point in lying. She was indeed a stone heavier since Christmas and it showed.

Jimmy pressed his lips together and frowned.

'I'll cut out the pints,' she said. 'I'll soon be down again with a bit of exercise.'

'Yerra, what harm? I'm almost twelve myself, I have to lost the best part of a stone before Killeagh. But you'd be a lot more use to me at nine and a half today.'

'Why?'

'The Strand has some heat in her leg. She gave it an old bash off a pole up in Mallow and I had her off work for a few days. She looked fit enough then, so I've had a young lad up on her since. I'm in two minds now whether to keep working her or lay her off for another couple of weeks. It would've helped to put a lightweight up on her for the next few days till we see if the heat comes back.'

'I hope it's not serious.'

'Yerra it's a strange aul bollax of a thing. She's not lame on it at all, not since the second day, but any bit of work and it swells up with the heat.'

'What does Con think?'

'He's waiting to see now when we come back in.'

Celia felt the familiar excitement as Jimmy led Southerly Strand out of her box and paused to check the bandage on her foreleg. This was what made it worthwhile to struggle out of bed in the dark and stand shivering in an icy kitchen, then walk half a mile up a frosty boreen. This animal, and the work they would do together over the next hour.

She stroked Strand's nose.

'Hey there! Remember me?'

Jimmy caught her eye for a brief moment then zipped up his jacket with unnecessary force and stood beside the mare waiting with obvious impatience to give Celia a leg-up.

It was a busy morning. After working Southerly Strand and Bally C Lady Celia helped Jimmy and Con to re-build the jump at the top of the field and splashed whitewash on the boards at its side. It was a satisfying task, and Con assured her that their efforts had made it look just like a real point-to-point jump.

Con had left a pot of potatoes on the boil for his dinner. Back in the kitchen he cut thick slices of fat bacon from a cold joint and slapped one slice and three floury potatoes on to each plate, and carried the plates and the cutlery through to the front room.

Jimmy had been studying the racing pages of the *Examiner* while Celia looked out of the window, both expecting Con to produce the usual cup of tea. They stared at the irresistible plates that he was handing them.

'Jeez, Con, I'll be putting on a stone, not taking it off,' said Jimmy as he sat down at the table.

'You shouldn't have,' said Celia, her eyes lighting up at the sight of the steaming potatoes.

'Ye've six days to Killer,' said Con. 'Ye've plenty of time to go starving yerself.'

'It's a fucking late start to the season,' said Jimmy.

'Them bollax,' said Con, and he and Jimmy talked National Hunt politics between mouthfuls while Celia piously ignored the slab of yellow butter sitting in a dish beside her elbow.

Next morning she overslept. It was only a ten-minute doze, but it put her far enough behind schedule to make her cancel the usual snack of tea and soda bread, and rush straight out to her car.

It was covered in hoar-frost. She scraped a small hole clear on the driver's window and struggled impatiently with the almost-frozen door lock. Then she turned the ignition key and stamped on the accelerator. The engine fired once and missed. She gave it more choke and her heart sank as the noise from under the bonnet turned into a sick moan. She counted up to sixty twice then tried again. This time the noise was even more feeble.

A flat battery.

'Oh shit!' She had never yet been late, and the idea sent her into a panic. It would take well over half an hour to walk, even at the pace of a forced march, and Jimmy and Con would be off round the roads by the time she arrived. But that seemed to be the only thing to do.

She made one last attempt to start the car. This time the engine would hardly turn over at all. She pushed down her door handle with an angry sigh, as someone pulled it open from the other side.

'Ye've a flat battery there,' Barney Mack was growling at her. He was the last person she wanted to see.

'I know.'

He shuffled sideways, crab-like, looking at the ground, and waved her towards his car.

'I'll give 'oo a spin.'

'Will you? Okay, thanks, that'd be great . . .'

He picked up the galvanised bucket, which he had been about to fill at the water tap, and Celia sat in the passenger seat on a bit of sacking. When Barney Mack had coped with a short fit of coughing he turned the car and they headed off to Con's place.

'You can drop me at the top of the boreen if you like,' said Celia. 'I'll walk the rest of it.'

'Yerra, go 'way.'

'You might get stuck.'

'Tis nearly froze over.'

They made it to the yard without sticking and Celia waited as Barney Mack turned his car. Then she opened her door.

'Thank you very much,' she said, wishing she could let him know how grateful she was.

'Go 'way. Give me a loana them keys.'

His big gnarled hand trembled slightly as he held it out to her, then his fingers closed awkwardly around her car keys as she dropped them into his palm. There was no time for questions or arguments. She could see Southerly Strand in her box already tacked up. That meant she was keeping Jimmy waiting.

The frost was still on the ground at half past ten as Celia and Jimmy finished work in the field. It was only when they were approaching Con's house that she saw her car parked outside it. Barney Mack got out of the driver's seat and gave her a wave.

She walked Bally C Lady down to him and dismounted.

'You've got it going! That's terrific. Thank you . . .'

'I give 'oo the loan of a battery. I've yer own on charge above. And ye've clean plugs and points. She'll give 'oo no more trouble for a while now.'

'Barney . . .' It was the longest speech he had ever made to her, and she was stuck for words. But the expression on her face said it all, and she noticed that his eyes, underneath their shaggy brows, were looking almost as pleased as she was feeling.

'Will you have a cup of tea with us, then I'll give you a spin back?'

He nodded and shuffled round to Con's back door.

When Celia caught up with Jimmy in the yard she shouted, 'He's fixed my car! Isn't he great?'

'He is a'course,' said Jimmy. 'He's a genius with anything mechanical.'

'But I never even asked him. He didn't have to.'

Jimmy handed her a net of hay for the Strand and spoke in the impatient tone of voice which always made her feel stupid.

'A'course he didn't have to. He's fond of you, he think's you're one of our own, that means he'd give you an arm and a leg if he thought it would help you. He's a fine man.'

'Well I know that now, but I've only just found out.' She was humbled by his kindness, and her previous superficial judgement of Barney Mack made her feel very small. 'How can I thank him?'

Jimmy thought it was only fair to Barney Mack to give her a straight answer: 'Bake him a cake.'

'A cake!' She had a suspicion that Jimmy was being sarcastic.

'He lives on the shagging stuff. Cake and tea and porter and one square meal a week with Peg Leary on Sundays. He'd get more nourishment from one of your cakes than he does from a dozen shop cakes.'

'I'll bake him a cake every week,' said Celia, and she meant it.

'So who's coming to the races?' asked Celia. 'There's three spare seats going in my car.' She was taking Lily, and Jimmy had suggested that Lily would be more comfortable in her car than in the draughty Land Rover. Celia would have preferred to travel with the horses, but she was also keen to give Lily a nice time. Having committed herself to taking the car, she now wanted to fill it up and make a real outing of it.

'No way,' said Ben. 'I've been to one point-to-point and that'll last me a lifetime. No shelter, no goddamn bar. Take your own booze and piss in the bushes. You gotta be cracked to drive three hours for that.'

'I agree,' said Emily. 'It's just cold, wet and primitive. And extremely dangerous. A spectator got kicked in the head by a loose horse at the last one I went to and he was carted off in an ambulance. No thank you.'

'Daniel, what about you? I've made a great picnic. Game pie.'

'I've not been to the races since I was ten years old. The Killarney races, and the parents lost me in the crowd. I had a great time.'

'I've never been,' said Fanny.

'That's it so.' Daniel had decided. 'If you've room for the three of us I'll take Fanny and Ownie to the races and we'll make a day of it.'

Ownie started to protest in his quiet way. He had studying to do.

'Bring yer aul books along with you,' said Daniel. 'And we'll drop the two of yeeze back at school after the races. Then I'll take off on a spree with Lily and Celia.'

This last idea did not fit in with Celia's plans, but she was happy to be taking the three Macarthys. Fanny and Ownie were nice kids, and apart from occasional Saturday nights in

Lily's, they did not seem to get out much when they were at home.

She left them to begin the Saturday night poker game and took her drink to the bar where Jimmy was standing next to Con.

'Aren't you going gambling with your friends?' said Jimmy.

She shook her head. The expenses of tomorrow's petrol and picnic had left her very little to gamble with, and she was saving that for the horses.

'Run out of luck, eh?' Jimmy smiled at her.

Celia found his attitude hard to understand. He was friendly, but only in a remote, rather impersonal way. At times she was aware of a new tension in him. He kept giving her strange looks, and she was not sure how to interpret them. It was as if he wanted to say something to her, but could not quite bring himself to do it.

The renewed daily contact with Jimmy had made her anger at what she now thought of as his 'little fling' with Clarissa evaporate. If indeed he had fucked her in the moonlight on the strand out at Ardbeigh, then it was a gloriously typical piece of bravado. And, Celia now imagined, he'd probably treated the whole episode as a bit of a joke. He may even have had a bet with Con about it.

Celia accepted her new affection for Jimmy quite calmly. It was different from the first weeks of all-absorbing passion which had contained, she now realised, certain implicit long-term expectations. This time it really was a friendly affection and if, as she intended, she managed to get him into bed again, this time she would be able to do so with detachment, expecting nothing more than just a bit of company. As he'd put it at the start: 'a nice warm body in the bed on a cold winter night'. That was enough, she'd settle for that.

Meanwhile she spent as much time as she could in his company, waiting for that moment of vulnerability which would allow her to suggest adding a physical side to their re-established friendship. Perhaps tomorrow, if they had a win at the point-to-point, or even a place . . .

Her interest in the conversation between Jimmy and Con on her left picked up at the mention of Southerly Strand.

'Will we run her tomorrow, what d'ye say?' Jimmy asked Con.

'We will, boy, we will. She's sound enough on that aul leg.'

'I'd say she's a good chance of a place.'

'She has. And she's worth that much more to ye as a brood mare if she's a few races won.'

'Oh aye. And we'll give Bally C Lady a spin too.'

'We've them both entered and we'll run them both. The Lady could use the outing to get a bit more schooling over the sticks. But ye're taking a risk with the Strand. She may well break down.'

'She may. But if she does we'll keep her as a brood mare.'

'So we'll run her till she breaks down, and then we'll put a horse into her,' said Con triumphantly.

'We will so,' said Jimmy. It was the conclusion of many hours of conversation at Con's table to which Celia had been a silent witness, and she felt as elated as they did at the mare's reprieve from the knackers.

It was time for last orders. Celia took her leave of Jimmy and Con, saying she'd see them out at the yard next morning at seven, and caught Lily before she disappeared to reassure her that she'd be picked up at a quarter to ten. Then she went into the back room where the poker game was still going strong. She pulled a chair up to wait for a chance to fix a time and place to meet the Macarthys.

Emily was fed up with the long arguments between Daniel and Ben about the carefully established house rules, and had dropped out of the game. She turned to Celia.

'How're you keeping? I don't seem to see much of you these days.'

'I've been busy with the horses. And you?'

'Stinking cold.'

'I thought you didn't get colds.'

'Well I've got one now.' She sniffed noisily, then pulled a handkerchief out of her sleeve and blew her nose. 'I suppose you've heard that Jimmy's buying *Château Despair?*'

'No, I haven't.' Maybe, thought Celia, he'd let her live in the caravan when the lease on her house was up.

'Mmmm. He's towing it up to one of Con's fields next week. And I've a good offer for my land.'

'That's great.'

'It is. It all depends now on what I can get for the house. It could take years to shift that. Anyway, I think I'll be sharing Clarissa's place at first while I take a look around. It's one hell of a complicated business.'

'I suppose it must be.'

'How's things with the half-sir?'

Celia sighed. 'Well, at least we're on speaking terms. Strictly business, but quite amiable.'

'Ah, well, that'll sort itself out soon enough.'

'How do you know?'

'It will a'course. You two were made for each other.'

Celia was greatly cheered by that remark.

Emily stood up and pulled on her coat, hat, scarf and gloves as Pake started to roar '*Time now ladies and gentlemen PLEASE. Have yeze no HOMES to go to?*' and left Celia to make her arrangements with Daniel.

Celia was out at the yard before seven next morning to lend a hand with the grooming. She and Jimmy had already made one attack on the mud-caked coats after riding out on Saturday, but the animals needed another half-hour's work. Celia had brought Bally C Lady up to the yard and was working on her in the box adjoining Southerly Strand's.

'How's it going there?' called Jimmy over the tall partition.

Celia was still sending up dust from the mare's rump. A cloud of motes shimmered in the dim electric light.

'Slow work.'

'Don't worry yourself too much. I tell you one prize we'll never win, and that's for the best turned out horse.'

He stood on the edge of the Strand's water bucket and looked down at Celia.

'That'll do now. Just comb her tail through as best you can then we'll give them a manicure out in the yard.'

Con turned up while Jimmy was painting oil on to Bally C Lady's hoofs.

'Ye've done a grand job,' he said. 'They'll have the country robbed by their looks.'

Celia led the mare back into the box. As she came out into the yard Con grabbed her around the waist and lifted her off her feet.

'Who's a fine gerral?' he shouted.

'Con!' she screamed, and kicked her legs in the air. Jimmy turned and smiled at them.

'Put me *down*.' Celia was laughing. Con stumbled forward a few steps and dropped her on top of a couple of hay bales. Jimmy stretched out a hand to pull her back to her feet.

'Yer a holy terror Con Leary. Look at the state of our head-lad.' Jimmy looked at Celia, still with a great warm smile on his face, and picked a few pieces of straw out of her hair then brushed some more off her shoulders. She glowed, and then, in the cold morning half-light, she blushed.

'Come on in now and have a quick cup of tea before we get on the road,' said Con. 'We've a long aul day ahead of us.'

Celia and Jimmy had renewed the repairs to the lane so that she could drive up to the yard without getting stuck. It was her task to take Con down to Bally C in time for eight o'clock Mass, then go back to give Jimmy a hand loading up the horses. Jimmy would then pick Con and Barney Mack up after Mass and drive on to Killeagh.

When she got back from the church she was disappointed to find that Jimmy already had the mares loaded into a double horse box, and the box hitched on to his Land Rover. She had never loaded a horse into a box, and she wanted to learn how it was done.

Jimmy was checking the gear in the back of his car, rummaging about on the floor, throwing a tangle of stuff about on the seat.

'Shin boots,' he said as Celia came up to him. 'Did I put in the shin boots? Oh aye, here's one of them, bandages, bridle, martingale, colours, crash helmet, my boots, saddle, another shin boot, leathers, spare girth . . . leading rein, did I put in a leading rein?'

She had never seen him in such a state of confusion.

'Look, we've got a bit of time before the Mass ends. Why don't you lay it all out in the yard here and we'll double-check it?'

Five minutes later she stood and watched Jimmy drive out of the yard, and although he couldn't see her, she waved and made thumbs-up signs at the back of the horse box.

Jimmy had allowed four hours for the drive to Killeagh. Celia hoped to make it in three or less.

The poker game had continued up at Dromderrig House until the small hours and the three Macarthys fell asleep in the back seat before Celia had reached Skibbereen. Lily's knitting needles clicked away as Celia enjoyed the novelty of a long drive through the traffic-free Sunday roads.

Killeagh was on the other side of Cork city, off the main Cork to Dublin road. It was the first time Celia had been to Cork since moving to Bally C. She had imagined she would be going up about once a month, but even though she'd been offered lifts by Ben and Jimmy, it never seemed worth the effort. She looked without interest at the shops and wondered why she had ever thought she'd miss them.

They came to Killeagh sooner than she'd expected, and followed a red and white sign pointing off to the right: 'To the Races'. After turning down small lanes at two more signs, they joined a queue of battered muddy cars and paid a £3 entry fee to a man in yellow oilskins.

As the queue edged forward Lily opened her handbag and tapped Celia on the shoulder, handing over four pound notes.

'Get a couple of race cards as well, my dear.'

'No, Lily, don't worry, this one's on me.'

'I won't hear of it. 'Tis your car and your petrol and your picnic and I'm having a grand day out.'

'Well, thank you.'

'Doesn't look much like picnicking weather,' said Daniel, and he yawned.

The weather had got steadily worse on the drive east. Showers of sleet had fallen, and the overcast sky threatened more of the same.

'I'm supposed to park near the horse box so we can all eat in the Land Rover.'

'How do you know they've arrived?' asked Fanny.

'We took the same road and I didn't overtake them.'

Celia was waved into the field by another man in yellow. A third man in yellow waved her towards a parking space. She rolled down her window and shouted, 'I'm with a horse box.' He nodded and pointed her towards a gap in the hedge.

Celia braked on top of a grassy ridge and they looked down at a semi-circle of horse boxes of various sizes inside a large roped-off enclosure.

'Can you see a gap in the rope?' asked Celia.

'No.'

'Well, could you nip out and lift the rope while I drive

under it? I can see Jimmy's box down there on the right, and I think that's Bally C Lady being walked around below.'

'Where's the race track?' asked Ownie.

'It's up on the other side of that hill,' said Lily, pointing straight ahead of them. 'There's the parade ring on the left and you can just see the bookies and a few chip vans on the right there.'

Celia drove down to Jimmy's box and parked beside it.

'Hallo there.' Jimmy opened Lily's door and he and Barney Mack put their heads into the car. 'Lily, I hope you're well wrapped up. It's bitter cold.'

'I am, boy, no feara that. And I've my umb-e-r-ella in the bag.'

'Anyone like a cup of coffee?' asked Celia, opening her door to fetch the flasks from the back.

'I won't my dear. I'll go up and take a look at the crowds to stretch my legs.'

Lily tied on a rain bonnet and opened her door. Con, who had joined Jimmy beside the car, handed her out.

'Don't go losing your shirt above, gerral.'

'No feara that Con Leary. Its not your aul bagga bones I'll be putting my hard-earned money on.'

Con laughed and held Lily's large handbag while she opened her umbrella and pulled on her gloves. Then Barney Mack walked her up the hill.

Jimmy sat in the car in Lily's place. The windows began to mist up with steam from the coffee and his wet clothing.

'She's a great old character,' he said. 'You won't get another sight of her now till the last race is over.'

'What does she do?' asked Celia.

'Yerra, she'll bump into some old biddies and go back to their box or their car for the afternoon. Lily knows a rake of people around. She takes no notice of the horses, she's only here for the crack.'

'When do the races start?' asked Daniel.

'Twelve forty-five. They're on their way up to the ring

now. We're running in the third and the fourth so we've an hour to wait till the third. That's Bally C Lady.'

'Let's go up and take a look round,' said Daniel.

They all gathered around the back of the car to sort out their coats and gum boots.

'Where will we find you?' asked Daniel when they were ready.

'We'll be back at the box in half an hour or so,' said Jimmy.

Bally C Lady was being walked by her jockey, a young cousin of Jimmy's called Robert. Jimmy took Celia over to meet him, and she liked him straight away. He was a younger, smaller version of Jimmy. He and Celia had a quick chat about the mare's fitness, and Robert commented on how full of herself she was today: 'She knows she's going to run, and she loves every minute of it – the grooming, the box and all. She's leaping out of her skin already.'

Robert's father, the trainer from Mallow, had a horse running in the first race, and all three were keen to watch, so Robert loaded Bally C Lady back into the box. It looked easy enough to Celia: he just led her to the ramp and she walked in by herself.

Up at the top of the hill they were hit by an icy blast of wind. Celia stopped for a minute to zip up her jacket and when she looked up Jimmy and Robert were gone. She was surrounded on all sides by a mass of unfamiliar faces, all of them ruddy from the bitter cold. She made her way to a clearing in the crowd and looked down at the track below, which was marked out by red and white flags with bales of hay at the corners. Even from that distance the jumps looked enormous.

It was fun, being alone in a big crowd, hearing unfamiliar accents from Kerry and Limerick and Tipperary and knowing that somewhere in among the crowd were at least eight familiar faces. She pushed her way towards the ring, and hung about the entrance where horses were still making their way in.

Jimmy and Robert were in the centre of the ring talking to an older man, probably the uncle. Celia was not sure whether she would be challenged by some official if she tried to join them, so instead she decided to go and have a closer look at the bookies and the crowd.

There were two long rows of bookies standing on tea chests facing each other, with sunshades and vast multi-coloured umbrellas stuck up behind them. Each man had a large carpet bag slung from a post in front of him, and a small blackboard beside it. The whole event had a look of cheerful improvisation. She stood in between the two rows of bookies and watched the punters crowding in at different points waving fists full of notes as new odds were chalked up on the boards.

She heard over the Tannoy that the horses entered for the first race were going down to the start and she walked back to the ring in time to see the backs of the last four jockeys in their brightly-coloured silks as they headed off towards the course. Once free of the crowd, the horses went on at a slow canter and Celia watched them moving across the dark wintry landscape towards the start of the three mile course with excitement. Soon it would be Bally C Lady and Robert heading down there, then Jimmy and the Strand . . .

She was staring into the distance and had not noticed Jimmy and Robert waving at her.

'Come on down to the last jump. We'll get a good enough view from there and we'll be outa this fucking wind.'

She scrambled down the hillside behind them and climbed over a bank to the edge of the track. Once out of the wind, the air was comparatively mild, though a mizzle of sleety rain was falling.

'The goin'll be shit by the fourth race,' said Jimmy. 'Have you any goggles with you?'

'I haven't. I lost them last season,' said Robert.

'Me too . . . here they come!'

It was great to be so close to the track that you could feel the vibration from the pounding of the galloping hoofs and hear the splatters of flying mud. Celia's fists were clenched as the first two horses cleared the fence, then a group of them crashed through the birch leaving one rider behind, and, just as Celia was relaxing again, three stragglers came over to a great shout of encouragement from the crowd.

'The favourite's second last,' said Jimmy. 'He's making a complete bollax of it, that Hourigan.'

The unseated jockey from the second batch of horses got to his feet. He was caked with mud down one side, and walked towards them as he pulled off his crash helmet.

'Seanie! What did she do, fall asleep on you?' shouted Robert.

'Yerra fuck it. I made a right balls of it altogether.'

'Hourigan's way back in the field.'

'Yerra he's a right bollax of a pilot . . . did ya see if they caught the mare?'

'They have her below.' Robert pointed down the track.

'See yeez later,' and he walked away a little stiffly towards his lost mare.

The horse that they were interested in was pulled up after the second circuit and they watched the final circuit of the race in silence. Only five horses out of fourteen finished the course. Jimmy was looking worried.

'I'm wondering should we run the Lady at all. She hasn't a hope in hell over this ground.'

'We'll give her a spin in any case,' said Robert. 'If she tires I'll pull her up after the first circuit.'

Jimmy wasn't convinced. 'We'll check with Con.'

'What about the Strand?' asked Celia.

'She's fond of the heavy going, she'll do all right, I'd say. At least we'll find out now, at the start of the season, if she's going to go lame on us, and we can send her for a brood mare and bring on Ardbeigh Prince instead of wasting any more time on her.'

'My father says you're being hasty with her,' said Robert.

'Your old man's too cautious by far,' said Jimmy. 'You'll never have a winner unless you take a risk from time to time.'

Robert did not point out that his father had had many winners, and Jimmy as yet had had none. He knew that Jimmy's nerves, like his own, were stretched taut before a race, though neither of them would ever admit it, and it was not the time to go in for contentious discussion.

They caught up with Con back at the box.

'The bookies are having a grand day out,' he said.

'Oh aye. That Hourigan's a useless bloody pilot,' said Jimmy, then he added, 'It's heavy going for the Lady. Do you think we should run her?'

'Yerra what harm? We'll give her a spin now that she's here and pull her up after the first circuit.'

The mare was unloaded from the box once again, this time in company with Southerly Strand. Con walked the Lady and Celia took the Strand while Jimmy and Robert got changed. The next hour passed in a flash with everyone kept busy preparing the horses.

Celia had never seen the mares so excited. As Robert had said earlier, they were leaping out of their skins. It took the best efforts of the three men to get Bally C Lady tacked up. Celia kept well out of the way as the mare pranced from side to side, throwing her head around, and was greatly relieved not to be the one to have to get up on her back today.

Jimmy put the Strand back into the box so that the four of them could go up to watch the race. This time they all went into the ring, and Celia stood in the middle with Jimmy while Con walked the Lady around the edge. The mare was looking great. In Celia's eyes no other animal in the ring could compare with her.

Robert was looking almost as keen as the mare, hopping from one foot to the other and tapping his crop against his boot.

'Luck to ya boy,' said Con, as he gave Robert a leg-up.

'Good luck.'

'Luck.'

Robert nodded at them from the saddle and gathered up his reins. They watched his back disappear as he left the ring and took the Lady down to the start at a slow canter.

The Macarthys had spotted the group in the ring, and Celia stopped to talk to them as she left.

'Is Con's mare going to win?' asked Daniel.

She shook her head and put a finger on her lips, then said quietly, 'The going's too heavy for her. He'll be pulling her up after the first circuit.'

'So I can save my money.'

'Oh aye. But the Strand's worth a fiver in the next race. Southerly Strand. You might put a fiver on for me too, I doubt I'll get a chance to go up to the bookies.' She pulled a note out of her pocket.

'The bookies are great crack,' said Ownie. 'We've been watching them chalking up the odds.'

'When are we going to eat?' asked Daniel.

'After the next race. Jimmy won't eat before.'

'It's freezing, isn't it?' Fanny blew on her hands.

'Bit nippy. It's much warmer down where we're going to watch the race from. We'll be out of the wind. Come on.'

The Macarthys followed Celia down to the track. This time she had eyes for nothing but Con's green and white colours on Robert's back. She could not distinguish them at all until the Lady was at the second last fence of the first circuit. She was running about ninth or tenth and even Celia could tell that the mare was already tiring.

'*Pullerup boy*,' bellowed Con as she jumped the fence in front of them, and Robert slowed her and, when the rest of the field had passed by him, turned her into the middle of the track and trotted her in a wide circle. Jimmy, Con and Celia ran over to him.

'No fault boy,' shouted Con. ''Twas way too sticky for her.'

'Ah, she's a dote,' said Robert. 'She's grand steering too. And good brakes.' Robert patted the mare's steaming neck.

'And she's still sound,' said Jimmy.

As they approached their box they could hear Southerly Strand whinnying and fidgeting. The Lady whinnied in reply and the fidgeting stopped.

'They're fond of each other, that pair,' said Robert.

'Oh aye. And the Strand knows it's her turn next,' said Jimmy. 'She thrives on it.'

In no time at all, it seemed to Celia, she was walking up to the ring again, this time with Jimmy in Con's colours and Robert leading Southerly Strand. Con was still looking after his mare, and was meeting them down at the last jump.

'She's sound enough on that aul leg,' said Robert.

'She is. You'd hardly notice the swelling at all, and there's been no heat in it for the past week now.' Jimmy was more curt than usual, the only sign of his tension.

He and Celia stood in the middle of the ring as Robert paraded Southerly Strand around its edge.

'You can do that for me next week if you're able,' said Jimmy.

'I'd love to.'

'In your jacket and breeches with your hair in a bun.'

'In my yellow oilskins if it's anything like today.'

The voice on the Tannoy was instructing the jockeys to take up their mounts. Jimmy unbuckled his watch and handed the watch and his heavy jacket to Celia in silence. For the first time that day Celia felt a stab of fear, as strong as if someone had suggested that she ride the mare instead of Jimmy. This was a crazy game. People got killed riding in point-to-points. But she also understood why he had to take the risk, and the fear turned to pure excitement. After long weeks of work Southerly Strand was being given a chance to prove herself a winner. And Jimmy would be all right, she was sure of that.

She walked out of the ring with Robert, after watching Jimmy and the Strand set off for the start.

'He's stone-mad that cousin of mine. He shoulda brought on the bay and left the mare on light work for another month.'

'But if she breaks down he'll send her for a brood mare.'

'It's not a risk he had to take. I tell you, he's stone-mad.' Robert laughed. 'Then again, he might have a winner. She's that fit. I'd say she's worth a fiver – I'll see you down at the track.'

Celia made her way to the last jump where the Macarthys, Con and Barney Mack were already waiting. Robert caught up with them as the race was starting.

'For fucksake, seven of us, and not one pair of glasses between us,' he said. 'And I've a grand pair sitting at home idle when they should be here with me earning their keep.'

'*. . . and they're off to a good start, it's Golden Perfume in the lead from Down All the Coves and Knocksmall Star, with Southerly Strand going well on the inside . . .*'

'The Strand!' shouted Celia.

'Where are they?' asked Ownie.

'Coming up to the back straight. We'll see them in a minute.'

'*And it's Southerly Strand by a short head from Golden Perfume . . . Southerly Strand in the lead as they come to the fourth fence . . .*'

All seven of them were shouting by the time Southerly Strand jumped the fence in front of them, still in the lead. Celia had both her fingers crossed and was jumping up and down.

'*. . . and Golden Perfume is gaining ground as they take the second fence of the second circuit and . . . yes, Golden Perfume was the faller there, Golden Perfume has fallen, and its*

Southerly Strand from Knocksmall Star, Whojargappipi and Blackcastle Maid coming up now to challenge the leaders . . . Southerly Strand ridden by her owner Mister James Lordin is over safely and it's . . .'

'Come on Jimmy!'

'Yer nearly home boy!'

'Come on the Strand!'

The final circuit.

' . . . *and she's over the second last fence and its Southerly Strand still in the lead, Southerly Strand from . . . and Southerly Strand is gone, she's fallen on the flat, and now it's between . . .'*

'Jimmy!' It was a screech.

The group held their ground as one and looked back down the track to where Southerly Strand had fallen, some twenty yards before the last fence. Jimmy had been thrown over her head, and was curled up in a ball a few yards in front of the mare. The rest of the runners raced over and around the fallen mare and the tiny figure of her jockey. It seemed to take the field forever to get clear, then as Celia, Con and Robert started to run up the track, they saw Jimmy stand up, look around him, and start walking towards the mare.

'He's up! He's all right.'

'Look to the mare!' said Con. 'The mare's still down!'

Jimmy was kneeling at her head when they reached him.

'The vet!' he shouted. 'Fetch the bloody vet. She's in agony.'

Then Celia noticed that tears were pouring down Jimmy's distorted face, clearing a channel through the mud. Robert ran off towards a steward. Con knelt and loosened the mare's girth. Celia knelt next to Jimmy. He looked up at her through his tears, opened his mouth, then his head collapsed on to her shoulder with a great sob.

'Take him away outa that!' said Con roughly. 'I'll see to everything here.' His voice cracked. 'Take him away home in your car. I'll bring the box and the others.'

'But I thought you didn't . . . oh, the Strand!' Celia broke down too. She had looked into the mare's eyes, eyes that were pleading, uncomprehending . . .

'Gerraway outa this and take him with you, for God's sake woman, *now!*'

She pulled Jimmy to his feet and put an arm around his waist, brushing away her tears with her free hand. Jimmy stopped and unbuckled his crash helmet, then threw it with great force into the mud.

One of the crowd who had gathered around the fallen mare picked up the hat and handed it to Celia. She nodded her thanks and went on slowly up the hill with Jimmy leaning on her shoulder.

He didn't say anything until they reached Bandon over an hour later.

'It wasn't the bad leg at all, the one that broke.'

'I know.'

Half an hour later, in Clonakilty, he said, 'She ran a great race. She woulda won. And she was doing it all herself. I couldn't hold her back, she was out in front right from the start.'

In Skibbereen they stopped for a hot whiskey.

'There'll never be another one like her.'

'She was a beauty. And a great old character.'

'Oh aye. I broke her and I schooled her and I've never known a horse learn so fast. She loved her work. You remember how she ran away with you the first day you rode out?'

'Christ, I'll never forget. I was terrified.'

'Yerra we knew she'd stop soon enough if we held back ourselves. Once there's nothing chasing her she loses interest . . . oh, Jesus! I can't believe she's gone.'

'She'll be out of her pain at least.'

'And in to the knacker's van. What a way to start the

season. Christ, why do I have all the bad luck? I'll never look at another horse again. The bay and the gelding are up for sale.'

'You can't be serious.'

'I am. I'll never touch another horse as long as I live.'

'Will you have another one with me in Lily's?' he asked, as they drove into Bally C.

'I will a'course.'

They sat up at the bar, silent. Celia wanted to comfort Jimmy, but everything she could think of to say she rejected as trite, so she sat tongue-tied.

'What's the matter with you two? Lose your shirt at the races?'

Jimmy looked around at Ben and said slowly and unemotionally: 'I lost a mare. She broke a leg galloping on the flat and had to be destroyed.'

'Oh, Christ, I'm sorry, real sorry Jimmy. Pake! Two hot ones here.'

'Thanks.'

They drank steadily for the next two hours. Once the news got around the bar, drinks and condolences were offered from all sides.

'You've never seen me langers have you?' said Jimmy.

'No. Not really.'

'You will tonight.'

She smiled for the first time since the race.

'Don't look so cheerful,' he said. 'There'll be a third thing. I can't think what, but bad luck always comes in threes.'

'So you need two more.'

'No. Just the one.'

Daniel came into the bar. He shook Jimmy's hand and patted his back and mumbled condolences. Then he bought a round of drinks and disappeared into the back room.

Jimmy stared at the drinks and said, 'Con must be home then.'

'Do you want me to drive you up to the yard?'

'I do not. I don't want to look at another horse as long as I live. I'm giving it all up.'

Celia did not believe him, but neither did she argue. By now he was getting maudlin.

'Every time I let myself get fond of something I lose it. I loved that mare, dammit, and there'll never be another one like her.'

'–'

Lily appeared behind the counter and put her hand out to take a hold of Jimmy's.

'My dear, I'm so sorry. You've terrible luck altogether.'

'I have Lily, I have. First I lose Celia, then I lose the mare . . .'

Lily saw her chance. 'Yerra, you haven't lost Celia at all. She's sitting right there beside you.'

Celia put her arm around him and kissed his muddy cheek.

'You haven't lost me you know. I'm right here.'

'Terrible thing altogether,' said Lily, but she was smiling to herself as she moved away up the bar.

Celia slept at Jimmy's that night. He fell asleep as his head hit the pillow and didn't wake up until nine the next morning.

They made love silently, then lay beside each other holding hands.

'Celia. Thanks.'

'For what?'

'For looking after me. I was in a real state. And for stopping the night with me.'

'Jimmy.'

They were silent again, each looking for the best way to

say what was on their mind. Jimmy tried first:

'Do you think we could try again? Would you like that? Take it slowly this time, no falling in love and no messing?'

Celia considered. Jimmy was more complicated than she had thought. There was something cowardly or mean or both about the way that, in normal circumstances, he made such efforts to deny his natural feelings of affection. She didn't like that, and she didn't think it would ever change. It didn't stop her liking Jimmy as a friend, but it was enough to stop her getting sentimental about him, she reckoned. She doubted this would ever be a grand romantic passion, but meanwhile, meanwhile . . .

'Okay. Let's try again.'

'You're a grand girl Celia.' So matter of fact, damn it.

'Will you move up here to Bawnavota with me?'

Celia had not expected that invitation, at least not so soon. But in another month Jimmy would be starting work on her house in Bally C, and she liked the idea of moving up to Bawnavota straight away. Old Mrs Beatty's place had gone sour on her in the last couple of months.

'I will, so,' she said.

'And no messing.'

'There never was any messing. Ben explained that.'

'If you move in with me you're my woman, and I want that to be clear.'

Celia thought about this for a minute, then said: 'That means no messing on your side either.'

'There never was any messing. D'you think you left me any need for other women?' He seemed astonished at the very idea.

'So what about Clarissa?'

'Once. And that was before I started anything with you.'

'My god, we've been a right pair of eejits.'

'Haven't we just? A right pair.'

MARCH

March, and the furze was out, great clumps of yellow flowers brightening the hillsides. Primroses and wild violets were growing on the banks of Con's boreen and the first daffodils were in bud down in the shelter of his house. Celia had filled the kitchen at Bawnavota with bunches of pussy willow and assorted sticky twigs.

The move to Bawnavota and the sudden disappearance of winter gave Celia a new burst of energy. She rode out every morning on Bally C Lady. As she had predicted, it had taken Jimmy only two days after losing the mare to get back to his horses. Bally C Lady had run in three more point-to-points, and almost got a place on her last outing. There was talk of buying a hunter for Celia in the September sales.

Jimmy was working in Con's field schooling Ardbeigh Prince and the new bay. Sometimes Celia joined him there, sometimes she went off on her own or with Con to hack around the lanes. Afterwards there was always a cup of tea and a chat with Con, then down to the shops in Bally C and up to Bawnavota for lunch. Three afternoons a week Jimmy went into Skibbereen and occasionally he made a trip up to Cork.

As she had time on her hands in the afternoons, Celia was helping Jimmy to get his properties ready for the tourist season. As yet he had no bookings, but he was optimistic. She had cleaned out *Château Despair* (or the mobile home, as Jimmy insisted on calling it). Two rooms at the cottage beyond Ardbeigh needed painting, and after that she was going to get to work on old Mrs Beatty's place.

Lily and the Penny Farthing wanted pasties again from St Patrick's Day on, and she'd decided to start a vegetable patch of her own at Bawnavota. Barney Mack had already been over it twice with a rotavator and Jimmy was fencing it in to keep the dogs off. Daisy was due to have pups any day now and once they started running around the place, nothing would be safe.

Celia and Jimmy had immediately picked up on the companionable routine established before Christmas. Sharing a house simplified matters and suited both of them. Celia did all the cooking and Jimmy washed up. She was amused to discover that Peg Leary, Con's sister, came in once a week to clean for Jimmy. Celia had never had a cleaner before, and thought it was a very luxurious indulgence.

They were both tidy by nature, and both were used to doing things alone. Jimmy never read books, and was fond of watching sport on television which, unless it involved horses, bored Celia. She read books instead. He sometimes had to see clients in the evenings and when he did so she either stayed in or went down to Lily's by herself. If Jimmy went with her he usually stuck with Con and Barney Mack while she gossipped or played cards with Ben and Emily and the Macarthys.

It seemed to Celia that this way of living allowed them to keep the better things about living alone while escaping the moments of loneliness. She had pleasant company and a familiar lover, but there was no compulsion to form a symbiotic couple and live each other's lives.

'There's a grand stretch in the evenings now,' said Daniel.

'Oh aye. You'd notice the difference in the light,' said Celia, who was showing him her new vegetable patch. It was half past six and the sun was still up. 'It'll be summer before we know where we are,' she added.

Daniel stopped walking. 'That's what I wanted to talk to you about,' he said.

'Oh aye?' It had struck her as odd that he'd wanted to come out and look at a newly dug patch of earth. She had yet to plant anything.

'I'm thinking of opening a restaurant for the summer and I was wondering if you'd like to come in on it.'

'A restaurant!'

'Nothing too elaborate, just plain cooking, plenty of fish and salads, fresh local produce, that sort of line, maybe even some delicatessen stuff to take away. We could get a lease on Paul and Barry's place for six months, April to September, and if it worked out we could maybe keep it open for some of the week in the winter . . .'

She knew the place he was talking about. It had been a chic, rather expensive restaurant when she'd first visited Bally C with Liam, but had been 'To Let' for some years now. Daniel continued with his plans: 'It'll need a bit of redecorating, and we'll need some capital to set it up, we could go fifty-fifty on that, but I reckon we'll earn it back in the first season with a small profit to share. And when we're busy Marie would give a hand, and Fanny and Ownie.'

She wondered why he needed her in on it at all . . .

Capital. Of course. There had to be a snag.

'Now much capital?'

He named a modest sum.

'I haven't got it.'

'Jimmy has.'

'Ah.'

It would never have occurred to her to ask Jimmy for a loan. They never discussed money and she hadn't a clue about how little or how much he had. But she loved the idea of a restaurant, and if it were a sound business proposition, and if he had the money, she did not think Jimmy would refuse. It was a very exciting idea.

'Give me a few days,' she said. 'I want to wait for the right time to ask him. Don't say a word to him about it, okay?'

'Grand.'

Daisy had her pups two days later. She started to whelp by the fire in the kitchen and there was such a terrified look in her eyes that neither Jimmy nor Celia had the heart to move her out to the shed they had prepared.

Jimmy still scolded Celia for her 'softness' with the animals, but she ignored him. She knew by now that his sternness was only a façade. If anything, he was even more attached to them than she was.

'Will she be all right do you think?' Daisy was howling. It was her first litter of pups, and Jimmy had confessed that this would be the first time that he had witnessed a birth. Celia, whose family pet had often had pups, took charge, and sat on the floor beside Daisy stroking the bitch's head.

'I think she's okay. We'll just have to wait and see . . . look, it's coming out, the first one . . .'

'Oh my God.' Jimmy turned pale. Daisy leapt to her feet and then crouched down and growled at the tiny pup which lay on the hearth rug.

'It's all right Daisy, it's all right . . .' The bitch backed away with a low howl.

'Don't touch it,' said Celia. Jimmy had been about to pick up the pup and take it to its mother. 'She might reject it if it smells of human . . . here, Daisy, come here Daisy . . .' Celia picked up the placenta between thumb and finger and tempted Daisy back towards the pup. She sniffed suspiciously at the pup, then snatched the placenta out of Celia's fingers and swallowed it with a gulp.

'She's eaten it!' said Jimmy.

'She has a'course. That gives her energy for the next one. That was the placenta, you twit.' To Celia's great amusement Jimmy was looking sicker by the minute.

'Oh Jaysus.' Daisy was licking the wriggly pup clean. 'I think I'll leave you to it.' And he went down to Lily's.

When he came back ten snub-nosed pups were squirming around in a box of hay with the bitch sleeping beside them.

'I think they should stay in the kitchen tonight, don't you?' Celia was trying to sound brisk and unsentimental.

'Oh aye. Just for the one night.' Jimmy put his arm around Celia. 'You're a great little midwife.'

'Ten of them.'

'She was one of a litter of twelve.'

'Still, it's not bad for the first litter.'

'Oh no, not bad. Not bad at all.'

They left the pups and sat at their usual places, one on either side of the head of the table, with their feet stretched out to the hearth.

'How were things in Lily's?'

'Quiet. Barney Mack's up in the hospital with the 'flu.'

'Oh, poor thing. I'll go up and see him tomorrow and take him his cake. Do you think they'll let me?'

'They will a'course.' Jimmy liked the way that Celia had kept her word about Barney Mack's weekly cake.

'Was Daniel there?' she asked.

'No. Why?'

She repeated Daniel's restaurant idea to Jimmy, embellishing it with details of the menu and stressing its potential as an all-year-round operation. He seemed to be reacting well.

'I don't see why you shouldn't make a go of it. The two of you are great cooks, and you're both good organisers and reasonably hard workers.'

'There's just one problem.'

'What's that?'

'He wants me to put up half the capital.'

Jimmy smiled one of his sudden wide smiles.

'How much do you need?'

She named the sum.

'It's all yours.'

'Jimmy! Thanks, that's wonderful . . . why are you smiling like that?'

'Because it means you're staying with me. I've been wanting to loan you the money to do something on your own for weeks. Something steadier than the pasties, but I thought maybe you'd be offended . . .'

'Offended? Why?'

He was serious now: 'In case you thought I was trying to bribe you, to make you stay. That's why I offered to buy a hunter for you in the September sales, to see how you'd react, but you didn't seem to get the message. I've been worried sick you might suddenly decide to leave . . .'

'Leave? But I've never been happier in my life. Honestly, Jimmy, I've never felt so settled anywhere.'

They held hands across the table and stared at each other.

'I never thought I'd feel like this about anyone,' said Jimmy.

'Me neither.'

The pups were still in the kitchen a week later when Celia brought Emily up to Bawnavota for coffee. They bumped into each other in the supermarket, and Emily was delighted with the invitation. She had not been up to Bawnavota since Celia's move.

'Well, you've certainly made yourself at home here,' she said as she wandered around the kitchen. 'Where did you get all the daffodils?'

'Down at Con's place – as he says, "them fields is black with daffs". You must take a bunch away with you.'

'Oh, no thanks. That's the last thing I need. Clogheen is a disaster area at the moment. I'm trying to get packed up – can you imagine?'

'It must be awful.'

'Well, it is and it isn't. I'd got into a bit of a rut and I'm sort of looking forward to trying something new. I'll probably miss it like hell at first. I can hardly imagine not having the place, but at the same time now that I know it'll be off my back I'm feeling years younger.'

'You look it too.' Emily had hennaed her sandy hair and was wearing smart corduroy trousers and a bright red sweater.

'Clarissa took me shopping in Bristol.'

'How's she getting on?'

'Oh, still as weird as ever. Totally obsessed by one of her neighbours. She says he's a very good poet, but he doesn't *look* anything special. Kind of strong and silent. And he's even older than Ben.'

Celia laughed. 'Have you seen the pups? Ben's getting the pick of the litter.'

Emily went over to the box. 'Ah, they're sweet. Edward would love them.'

'Why don't you take one over for him?'

'Too complicated. I've already got his cat to worry about. You wouldn't take him for a while, would you, just till we get settled?'

'I don't know. We've already got a kitten. My old neighbour Mrs Harte talked me into it. They might not get on.'

'Oh, let's see.'

Celia went to the door and called the kitten's name. A white cat irregularly dotted with large black spots came pounding indoors and headed straight for Daisy's dish. Celia snatched the dish away and put it on top of the fridge. The cat squeaked and rubbed against her legs.

'That's a kitten?' said Emily. 'She's enormous. Absolutely extraordinary. She looks more like a Friesian cow than a cat.'

'Well, we think Petal's very sweet,' said Celia. 'Do you take milk?'

'Please. By the way, you must come up to Clogheen before the auctioneer and see if there's any stuff you can use for the restaurant.'

‘Thanks, that’ll be great. When’s the auction?’

‘Next month. Then the estate agent’s found a summer tenant, and if they like it they might make an offer. He’s dynamite, that estate agent.’

‘I know. Jimmy’s thinking of using him this year. He sounds very efficient.’

‘Quite amazing for Skibbereen.’

Celia walked over to the stove and stirred a pot of soup. ‘I’m doing tests for the restaurant,’ she said. ‘Daniel wants costings on everything. He’s being very professional about it all, he makes me feel a total amateur.’

‘Well, he’s done his time in the catering business. He keeps quiet about it but I’m sure he’s earned more money in catering than playing his damn guitar.’

‘Not that he has one at the moment. At least, no twelve-string.’

‘That was a dirty trick of Charlie’s. There’ll be hell to pay when he gets back. You do realise you’re going to need riot gear working with the Macarthys?’

Celia was not bothered by this aspect of her new venture. ‘Don’t worry,’ she said. ‘I’ll survive.’

One especially fine morning Celia was hacking back from Ardbeigh alone when she happened to stop beside the old tin mine above Southerly Strand, and look out to sea. She walked the Lady closer to the cliff. Below her, in the coves, the sea was grey, shading to a greeny turquoise until, beyond the islands, on the horizon, it turned dark blue. Between the coves and the islands there were crisp bursts of white foam at irregular intervals. The wind blew the Lady’s mane about, and she pawed the ground with her foreleg and fidgeted, a habit which still sometimes alarmed Celia.

It was low tide. Celia decided on pure impulse to take the mare down below for a gallop. It was the first time she had done this alone. She trotted the mare up to the far side of the cliff where a path sloped gently to the sea, and she walked her down to the firm sand at the water's edge. Then she turned the mare's head into the wind and kicked her on. First it was a steady canter, then the mare pulled and Celia gave her her head, letting out a shout as the Lady broke into a flat-out gallop. Sea, wind, mare, motion, speed, Celia were all one.

Only a short moment of panic – the rocks at the end of the cove came near so fast – would she stop, could Celia turn her in time, and if not . . . but she did. The mare knew the routine and responded to Celia's commands, turning in towards the cliff and trotting back up the strand.

Celia patted the Lady on the neck, and got her own breath back. She let the mare walk on at her own pace and relaxed into the saddle as she watched the small breakers on the shoreline foam white and disappear.

She lifted her eyes and stared across the bay, past the scattered islands to the horizon, and the sound of the out-haul reached her on the wind.

She laughed aloud. The out-haul said it all. She had no need of sweet words and promises from Jimmy. She had his friendship and his company, and this. Here on the strand with the sound of the out-haul it was possible to believe that there were no dark corners. Here there was beauty, and a continuity of life that made the rest seem petty and transitory. As long as she could listen to the out-haul Celia knew that she would be all right.